This story is dedicated to the memory of
Dad, Joanne and Maria.

Also to my children, Natasha, Adam and Sam,
who are my inspiration.

GW00696995

Acknowledgements.

I would like to thank Audrey Chamberlain and Peter Sillett for their help, patience and
hard work during the early days of this project.

Chapter index

One.

Bad Memories.

(Spring 2003)

'Dad, can we get chickens?' asks Peter my youngest son.
'What?'
'I said, can we get some chickens?'
'Are you mad? What do you want chickens for?' Bad memories from my childhood hit me, clear as newly blown glass. My parents kept chickens when my sister Sarah and I were very young. I hated the dirty birds.
'My teachers got chickens, she says they are good fun.'
'We can't keep chickens, we have no place to keep them. They're dirty animals.' I say, spitting out the words.
'I'd look after them,' said Peter. Putting his hands together as if begging. His eyes pleading from behind his

over long, golden fringe.

'Let your mother get chickens. You're only here at the weekends. I would have to look after them the rest of the week and that isn't going to happen. I've not got the time.'

'You'll get free eggs, Dad.'

'We can't have chickens, that's all there is to it!'. As an afterthought I added, 'The cat would eat the chickens.'

'Cats don't eat chickens,' retorts Peter. 'Farmers have always got cats. You said I could have a pet.' Peter's vibrant blue eyes are filling, as his voice trembles.

'You have Logan. We don't need another pet.'

'He's never here. As soon as we open the back door, he's gone,' Peter argued. 'Chickens stay in the garden and let you hold them.'

'No!' I shouted. 'They peck you and fly at you. They get you into trouble!'

'What do you mean "Get you into trouble?" Peter laughs. 'How can chickens get you into trouble?'

'We're not getting chickens, that's the last time we're going to talk about it,' I said, showing Peter who is the boss.

One month has passed and we are driving back from a poultry farm in Beaulieu. Boxed up on the back seat are Goldie and Molly. Peter is sat in the passenger seat, babbling with excitement and good intentions. Looking forward to his new excursion into animal husbandry.

A couple of nights later, I'm slumped on the bed thinking about my ex, Charlie. *Why couldn't we stay together? Because she's a nutter that's why. She was jealous of the children and everyone else. God, Charlie, I do love you.* I can't get her out of my thoughts. I reach for one of my happy pills on the bedside table, wash it down with a slurp of vodka. *Maybe that will help.* I'm finding it hard to sleep because it's an unusually warm April night. The lights off, my curtains open. I'm pondering what to do next. *Why did I take redundancy?* I have no idea what direction I'm going in. Then something catches the corner of my eye. I could not believe it. There, as plain as day, was a little flying lady. I'm going mad. She was the same angel I saw as a child. I had forgotten all about her. I'm stuck there frozen for a moment. Flying up to the window pane, she winked, then waved at me. Jumping from the bed, I run to the window. What I am seeing, I can only describe as a fairy. I remember thinking her an angel when I was a child. My memories are instantly shot back to childhood.

(Summer 1966)

It was early morning, the heat from the sun was just starting to a lift hazy dew from the lawn. My feet were bare, I could feel the damp grass between my toes. A spider was spinning a new web on my favourite bush. I called it the vinegar bush, because the dark red leaves tasted of vinegar when I chewed them.

'Would you let the chickens out?' Mum shouted from the house. I was five years old and had been scared of the chickens for as long as I could remember. They always flapped around and chased me.

'Can't Sarah do it? She's bigger than me, they don't peck her.'

'Sarah's gone to the butchers', mum replied. 'You'll have to do it.' I could feel the fear building up in me as I got closer to the chicken house. My heart started pounding like a sledgehammer deep inside my chest, my fingers tingled and my legs turned to jelly. The closer I got to the chicken coop, the smaller I became. The coop loomed above me like a vast wooden skyscraper. My hands were wet with sweat. I could hardly catch my breath as I reached to lift the shutter and let the feathered demons out.

'WHARK! WHARK! WHARK!' Out ran a pack of child hungry killer birds. I panicked and ran for the garden shed at light speed. Stumbling, I shot head first into the metal post of the washing line. CRACK! I laid in a daze just looking towards the sky, my head ringing like the bells on Christmas morning. As I started to come around, I saw a tiny flying lady. She was pretty. She sparkled like sugar frosting. From the house I heard my name shrieked.

'Alexander, are you tormenting those chickens again?' Looking to the house I saw my mother racing towards me with a large rolling pin. Turning back to the flying lady for help, she's no longer there. I was dragged back into the house and had to go without breakfast as punishment.

Late into the evening, my thoughts stayed with the little flying lady. *She must have been an angel.* I thought to myself. My father was sitting in his chair. He had the newspaper open on the racing page. Smoke from his pipe swirled around his balding head. His enormous, slippered feet on the foot stool.

'How big are angels?' I asked him.

'Don't ask me, your mother knows all about that stuff.' Dad shifted in his chair and shook the paper.

'I saw one today.'

'Saw one what?' Dad asked.

'An angel.'

'You had best go and tell your mum,' said Dad, looking uncomfortable. *Why don't dads know anything apart from football and horses?* Mum was still not happy with me. I sought her out. She was in the kitchen making Dad's packed lunch for the next day. She was wearing a clean pinafore. She was always neat and tidy.

'Mum, how big are angels? I saw one in the garden this morning. She was flying above my head, she smiled at me.'

'Don't be daft,' said mum. 'Angels don't fly around in the daytime, they visit people when they have a special message. The only things flying around your head today were the chickens. It's nearly bed time, get your night clothes on, I'll read you a story.' Then it hit me, bedtime. I just knew that I was going to have nightmares about the killer birds.

'Can I sleep in your bed tonight?' I pleaded. 'I'm scared!'

'Scared, scared of what?'

'The chickens.'

'The chickens, I've never heard such nonsense. Anyway, they're locked up for the night.'

'Please, Just this once, I promise.' That night I got my way and fell asleep to the sound of my father grumbling and my mother saying.

'You'll have to go without tonight dear.' Go without what? I wondered.

The next morning I 'woke early. I had a plan. It involved some special equipment. I opened the pantry door. An empty jar, that's what I needed. I knew that there were

5

some on the top shelf. I was too small to reach without the help of a chair. I dragged one across the kitchen floor. On tip toes, I reached up and grabbed a jar. It had the smell of pickled onions. Quickly, I put the jar up my jumper. As I stepped down, Sarah, my sister walked into the room.

'What are you doing?' She asked. 'You'd better not be pinching cakes, I'll tell Mum!'

'I'm not, I just need a jar.'

'You're not collecting worms again, are you?'

'No, I'm going to catch an angel. She lives at the bottom of the garden.' Sarah laughed. She was two years older than me and very clever. I expect she knew all about angels. 'Can you help me catch her?'

'No you little loony, I'm going out with Sally.'

'I'm not a loony! You're horrible.'

I'll do it myself. I had a jar. All I needed was my butterfly net. Angels are not much bigger than bugs. So with net and jar in hand and a cake in pocket. I set off down the garden path. I hurried past the hen house. I blew them a raspberry for good measure. At the very bottom of the garden was a potting shed full of dead plants and empty pots. A musty smell like damp dogs, always hung round the shed. A large family of spiders lived in there. I sought out a good spot to hide and wait. It was another sunny day, only one week into the school holidays. I was full of excitement. I just knew my angel would come back to see me. Hours passed. Nothing happened. I was getting real hungry. Then I remembered the cake in my pocket. I reached in, pulled out a crumbling mess with an elastic band and some fluff attached. Still, I ate as much of the cake as I could. Some of the crumbs fell to the ground, only to be quickly devoured by an army of ants. The crumbs must have been a banquet to them. It seemed like I'd been sat for ever. I could feel myself falling asleep. Dream images flitted in and out, ants on parade standing to attention.

'Left right, left right, left right,' screeched the biggest ant. They marched in unison, heads high, big smiles on their faces. I shook myself out of it. I would not catch my angel by falling asleep. I still felt drowsy, when I heard my name being spoken softly, sweetly. I looked up from the ants. There she was! My angel, flying just above my head. The sunlight caught in her wings, dancing with her. She was radiant. She was talking to me. She spoke in a whisper, I couldn't make out the words. That was my chance. I got up gingerly. Carefully, I reached for my net. She was fluttering and smiling. Quick as a flash, I swung the net to catch her.

'WHARK! WHARK!WHARK!'

'Oh no!' I'd caught a chicken.

'WHARK! WHARK! WHARK!' I tried to let it go but its feet got stuck in the net.

'WHARK! WHARK! WHARK!'

'Please be quiet, or mum will hear.'

'WHARK! WHARK! WHARK!'

'Alexander!' Mum screamed. 'What are you doing to those dammed birds now?'

'WHARK! WHARK! WHARK!'

'Please shut up. I'm trying to set you free.'

'WHARK! WHARK! WHARK!'

'OUCH!' My ear was stinging like mad: it was my mother, dragging me up towards the house. She was ranting and raving. I saw our neighbour, Mr Slate, looking over the garden wall and shaking his head.

'What do you think you're doing, tangling Henrietta up in your net!' Mother shouted.

'I didn't mean to. I was trying to catch an angel,' I said in my defence, tears streaming down my face.

'Stop all that angel nonsense!' Mother squawked. 'Bad boys don't see angels.' I was sent to my room for the rest of the day. Sobbing on my bed, I knew I had seen her. She was not a dream. She was real. But nobody would believe me.

(Spring 2003)

Why has she come back, after all these years? The flying lady was still just outside my window. As I opened the window, she shot off down the garden like a flaming arrow. She stopped, hovered over the chicken house, then disappeared. I run from the bedroom, down stairs, out of the back door into the garden. I'm searching everywhere for her. In and around the chicken house, under bushes, up trees. I don't know how long I've been searching. When I'm suddenly disturbed by a loud banging coming from the house. *Who could that be?* I run back up to the house. The banging is getting louder. There are voices, men's voices, at the front door. It then hit me, I was naked! I picked up a cushion from the sofa, on the way through the lounge. BANG! BANG! BANG!

'Open the door please sir.' BANG! BANG!BANG!

'Come along sir, open up. It's the police.'

The police! I wonder what on earth they could want at this time in the morning. Something's happened to one of my children. I was in a panic. BANG! BANG! BANG!

'We won't ask again,' said the voice. 'Open up now!'

I opened the door, cushion in front of me. I can feel my face turning crimson. At the door, stood two huge police officers. The younger of the two, is about six feet one. He has a barrel chest and a shock of flame-red hair. The older policeman isn't much smaller. He has a kindly face with a distinguished air about him. His silver grey hair adds to his sophistication.

'I'm Sergeant Ray, this is PC Smiley,' announces the older of the two. 'May we come in, sir?'

'Yes! Yes of course, what's happened?' I ask. I can see the younger officer, trying to stifle a laugh.

'Think we'd all better step inside, sir,' says Sergeant Ray.

'What's happened?' I ask again.

'Nothing to worry about sir,' replies PC Smiley. 'Just a complaint from one of your neighbours.' It then struck me that I'd been running round the garden, starkers, with nothing else but looking for fairies on my mind. I had to think fast, I could not use that as an excuse! I'd be locked up for sure.

'We have had reports of a man fitting your description, exposing himself in your garden,' says Smiley. My mind racing, trying to think of a convincing explanation for my behaviour.

'Intruders,' I say. 'Two blokes down the garden, I saw them from my bedroom window. Yes, intruders and I went down to confront them.'

'Did you catch them sir?' asked Sergeant Ray.

'No, they ran off.'

'They must have been scared off by your weapon, sir,' Smiley chipped in.

'I don't have a wea… Oh, very funny.'

'Do you often run about naked in your back garden sir?' asks Sergeant Ray.

'No, of course not. I just didn't think when I saw the men in the garden.'

'Have you been drinking, sir, or taking drugs?' asks Smiley.

'No! no, I was in bed when I was disturbed. I've not had a drink in days,' I lie. 'Do you mind if I put something on? I don't want my son or daughter coming home and seeing me like this.'

'I think we'd all prefer you to do so,' muses Smiley.

Rushing to the bedroom, two stairs at a time. I put on a pair of jeans and grab a T-shirt that was slung on the bed. As I returned to the lounge where the two officers are waiting, grins appeared on their faces. They are staring at my T-shirt. I looked down. Realising I couldn't have picked a worse shirt if I'd tried. In big, bold print is a quote from Shakespeare's, As You Like It:

"Though I look old, yet I am strong and lusty." I can feel my face burn with embarrassment.

'It was a present,' I say. 'From friends.'

'Can you describe what they looked like, these supposed intruders?' asks Smiley.

'Not supposed they were there. It was too dark, I couldn't see them properly. It all happened so quickly.' All this time, Sergeant Ray is writing in his pad.

'How many men did you say there were?' he asks.

'Two, yes, I'm sure I saw two of them.'

'Weren't you scared?' asks Smiley. 'Tackling two men on your own. It could have been dangerous.'

'I didn't think about the danger. It happened so quickly.'

All the time the questions are being asked. Smiley is scanning the room, obviously looking for some incriminating evidence.

'Where did you get those marks on your arms from?', asks Smiley. I look at my arms, grazed and bleeding. Smiley looks as though he has something against me. I've never met him before but he feels like an enemy.

'Must have done that on the bushes in the garden.' I reply.

'We'll give you the benefit of the doubt this time. If we get further reports of this sort of behaviour, we'll have to press charges. We won't keep you any longer sir,' says Sergeant Ray. 'Just try to be a bit more careful how you appear in public in future.'

'Oh, and if the intruders come back, give us a call,' says Smiley. 'Best left to the professionals.'

'We'll be off then, sir,' says Sergeant Ray.

'Perhaps you should get yourself a stiff drink,' says Smiley. 'You're obviously very cold.' I knew what he was getting at. The two officers made their way out.

'Good night and thank you,' I say. 'You'll have no more trouble from me.'

'Good night then, sir,' they say in unison.

I shut the door and walked back into the lounge. Taking Smiley's advice, I pour myself a vodka. I won't be able to sleep. So I put on a "Lou Reed" CD. Sitting in my favourite chair drinking, I question myself. *Why did you go and look for her? It was a dream. Fairies don't exist.*

'Yes we do!'

'Arrgh!' I scream, dropping my glass to the floor. 'Where did you come from? You're not real.'

Sat on the arm of the sofa opposite, is the fairy.

'Calm down, Alex.'

'You don't exist. You're not talking to me,' I cover my ears with my hands. 'La, la, la,la, you're not here. La, la, la, la.' I shout, pacing up and down my lounge.

'Stop it! I am real and you are going to listen to me.' Shouts the fairy. 'Just sit down. I will explain.'

'It's the vodka making me see things.'

'How can it be the vodka, you've only had a couple of sips.'

'Vodka goes straight too my head.'

'I've come to tell you that you need to go and see Sarah.'

'What? how do you know Sarah?'

'I know everything about you. I've been with you since you were five. Remember that day, in your garden. The day you tried to catch me in your net.'

'Yes, I caught a chicken and a sore ear from my mum. But you weren't real. No one else saw you. Why didn't you show yourself to my mum?'

'Grown up's don't see us.'

'I'm seeing you now.' The fairy laughs and puts her hand too her mouth.

'Well, you're an adult. But I wouldn't say that you're a grown up.'

'Insults as well.'

'Listen, I can't stay much longer....' I interrupt her.

'Please, don't let me keep you. I was doing Ok, 'till you came along.'

'I said listen,' she shouts. Slamming her microscopic hand down on the arm of the sofa, sending a minute plume of dust into the air. 'Achoo, excuse me,' she says, wiping her nose on her sleeve. 'You need to go and see Sarah. And when you get back, you need to give this place a good clean. It's a pigsty.'

'I can't just up and leave. What about the children?'

'Alex, your children are all pretty much adults now. I'm sure they could cope without you for a short while.'

'Why must I go to see Sarah, what's up?'

'Everything will become clear. Please, just do as I ask. Oh, and watch out for that Smiley, I don't trust him.' With that she disappears.

'Come back. I haven't finished talking to you.' I stay awake for the rest of the night, pacing up and down. Thinking about the fairy. The only time I saw her, as a child, was when I was near the chickens. There must be some connection. *I'm not going all the way to Cornwall, just because a fairy asked me too. Who the hell does she think she is.*

Two.

Reunion.

As soon as the doctor's surgery is open, I'm on the phone. I need more happy pills. Eventually I get through and receive the standard response.

'White Lane surgery, can I help you?'

'Yes, I'd like to make an appointment to see a doctor please.'

'Can I take your date of birth?'

'24th Feb 1961.'

'Can I get you to confirm your name?'

'Alex, Alexander Crain.'

'We can fit you in next Thursday Mr Crain, at 3.30pm, Dr Jenks.'

'Next Thursday, that's not soon enough. Have you nothing today?'

'Sorry Mr Crain, that's the soonest we can do.'

'Oh forget it.' I bark, slamming the phone down. Then pick it up again, franticly dialling.

'Come on, come on, answer the phone,' I'm still worried by the events of the night before. 'Come on, where are you? Answer the phone, for God's sake.' At last the phone's picked up.

'Hello.' It's Sarah, my sister, on the other end.

'Sarah, it's me, I need to see you. Can I come and stay for a little while?'

'Why, what's up, Alex?'

'I can't say over the phone. I just need to get away for a little while, just a week or two.' Silence falls for a brief moment.

'Of course you can. It would be nice to see you again. Has something happened?'

'No, nothing's wrong. I just need some time away from home.'

'Are you OK Alex? I know you're not working at the moment. Are you short of money? Do you need some cash?'

'I'm alright for money, nothing's wrong, I'd just like to see you.'

'Come whenever you want: you're always welcome,' says Sarah.

'Thanks, I'll be there later today.'

'Today! Oh…Ok that's fine. I'll get the spare room ready…'

After packing a small bag of clothes. I seek out James, my eldest son, he is in the kitchen.

'What time did you get in last night?' I ask.

'About three this morning, you were in the lounge pacing again. I thought I'd better leave you to it.'

'Just a bit restless. Keep thinking about Charlie, wish we could get back together.'

'Dad, you two were always arguing. Try and find some one new.'

'I'm going to visit Aunt Sarah for a while. Maybe the break will help me forget her.'

'Let's hope so, you're always up at night. You must be shattered.' James is an older version of Peter. He's more outgoing and self assured. But physically they are very much alike. Same blue eyes, fair hair and stocky body frame. I feel this is quite an achievement as they have different mothers. Makes me feel good about my genetic strength.

'Will you be gone long, dad?' James enquires.

'Not too long. I just need a change of scenery. Could you tell Jay and Peter that I've gone to see Aunt Sarah? Ask Peter to feed the cat and chickens while I'm away. I'm sure his mother won't mind dropping him round each day.' I knew that I couldn't ask James to do this. As he is always out and he doesn't like the cat much.

'No problem,' says James. 'Say "hello" to aunt Sarah and uncle Rob for me.'

'I'll see you when I get back. I've left some money in the kitchen. Don't spend it all on drink and parties.'

'You didn't have to do that! I've got some money,' says James.

'It's not compulsory to use it up, it's just in case you run out whilst I'm away. Right, I'm off. See you when I get back. I Love you. Tell Jay and Peter, I love them too. I'll phone you in a couple of days.'

'Bye, Dad. See you soon.' James looks at me anxiously.

I put my bags in the car. I'm only taking a couple of flight bags with me as I've not done the laundry yet. I check that I've got all I need. I have a quick slurp of vodka and a happy pill for the journey.

As I pull up at the petrol station, I notice it's empty. *Good, don't have to queue for petrol today.* The rush hour has just finished. I hate queuing for petrol. As I'm filling up, I notice the woman behind the counter. She's stunningly pretty. I'm a sucker for a cute face but I can't seem to deal with them anymore: I used to be able to chat anyone up. Now I stumble over my words like a jabbering fool. *Wow! She's waving at me.* I look behind me to make sure there's no younger man standing behind. *No, it's really me she's waving at!* I swell with pride. *You still got it, Alex.*

'Oy mate, I think you're full up.' The man at the next pump grabs my attention. Petrol is flooding out of the tank, down the side of the car and over my shoes. I feel stupid. That's why she was waving at me so frantically!

'I thought that these things were supposed to stop automatically,' I mumble embarrassedly.

'You've probably put a fiver's worth over the ground,' he says. I walk, shamefaced to the pay-point. The young woman just looks at me like I'm the village idiot. We say nothing to each other. I return to the car, drive off, the windows open and the blowers full on.

I'm heading out of the City on the Redbridge fly-over, when I spot a blue flashing light in the mirror. I pull to the side to let it pass. It's the police. They're pulling me over!

What have I done now? I paid for the petrol; it can't be speeding, I never speed. In the rear view mirror, I see a policeman get out the car and walk towards mine. Immediately I recognise him, it's Smiley, the young, arrogant, ginger-headed copper from last night. Then I remember what the fairy said.

"Watch out for Smiley."

'Good morning, sir,' grins Smiley, looking down at me. It doesn't take him long to recognise me.

'You again!' He smirks. 'Well, at least you're dressed this time. Don't think I could face a naked man at this time of the day. Did you know you've got a brake light out?'

'No. I'll get it fixed at the next garage I come across.'

'Could you step out of the car please sir?' Reluctantly I turn the engine off and get out.

'Where are you going?' he asks.

'Just off to visit my sister.'

'And where does this sister of yours live?'

'Why do you want to know?'

'Just answer the question.'

'I don't think it concerns you, where my sister lives.'

'This will all be much quicker if you just answer the question.' I can see that he's not going to give up, so I tell him.

'In Cornwall.'

'Do you think this car will make it to Cornwall?'

'Never let me down before.'

'Is that petrol I can smell? Is this car road-worthy, sir? May I see your licence?'

'I spilt petrol over myself. It's not leaking from the car.' Taking my licence from my wallet, I hand it to him. The licence is tatty, not in one piece.

'Thank you, sir,' says Smiley. He handles it like it's going to give him some sort of disease. 'It's about time you sent for a new one.' As he studies the licence, Smiley walks around the car. He kicks the front tyre, lifts one of the wiper blades from the windscreen and inspects it.

'These need replacing.' He continues his survey. 'This car's a pile of crap.'

'It's got another six months M O T left.' I say.

'That don't mean a thing. I'm going to need you to produce your papers at the station over the next couple of days.' Smiley fills out some paperwork and hands it to me. 'Bring this and your relevant papers to Bittern police station. And make sure you get that light fixed.' Smiley hands me back my licence and walks back to his car stretching, yawning, all the way. He turns and says. 'Just remember, I've got your number.'

I've a long journey ahead of me. I'm going to take the coast road, it's much nicer. Reaching for the glove compartment, I take out one of my happy pills, pop it in my mouth and swallow. I slip a "Bob Dylan" tape in the player, turn it up full blast.

"It ain't me babe, it ain't me you're looking for, babe." I'm tone deaf, but that doesn't stop me singing at the top of my voice.

As I drive through the New Forest, I think how nice it would be to live out this way. With the sun flickering through the leaves of the trees, the fresh smell and the large spaces between the houses. I'm just a country boy at heart. When we were young, we'd visit my aunts and uncles on my mother's side. They lived in Essex, in the small village of Navestock, a few miles outside Brentwood. I loved the woodland, the farms. Life in the country seemed to run at a much slower, more peaceful pace. My thoughts are disturbed by a bright light, glinting in the trees to the left of me. To my horror, it's the fairy. She's flying around in the woods. Slamming on the brakes. I jump out the car and race towards her. When I reach the wooded area where she was, I find nothing. No sign of her.

'Come out! Show yourself. What the fuck do you want now?' I stand in the thicket, listening. 'Why are you doing this? Why have you come back?' Behind me I hear laughing. Swinging around angrily, I shout. 'Leave me alone, just leave me alone!' The fairy appears again. Fluttering in the branches of an oak tree.

'Hi, thought I'd share a picnic with you,' she announces.

'You can't. I didn't bring one.'

'That's Ok, I did.'

'Why are you following me? You got what you wanted. I'm going to Sarah's.'

'Just want to make sure you get to where you are going.' She flutters down beside me. Throwing out her arms, she makes a picnic blanket appear. As it lands, an assortment of food fills it. Triangular sandwiches, pastry snacks, delicately decorated cakes and sparkling water.

'Will that do?' she asks.

'You forgot the pickled onions.'

'I don't do pickled onions, they upset me.' I find myself warming to her. If she is a dream, she's a pleasant one.

'What's your name?' I ask.

'Faith, pleased to meet you,' she teases, holding out her hand for me to shake.

Lifting my hand towards her, I offer her my index finger.

'Not sure if I'm pleased to meet you. But I have little choice.' As she touches my finger, I get a static shock. The electricity tingles through my hand.

'Shall we eat? I'm starved.' Faith flies over to one of the sandwiches and takes a nibble. I pick up a sandwich and take a bite. Savouring every second. I've not tasted any thing like it in my life.

'These are delicious. What's in them.' I ask, peeling the bread apart to investigate.

'That's a secret, a fairy secret.'

'You're good at keeping secrets. You still haven't told me why you want me to see Sarah.'

'Let's just say the visit will do you good.' I can see that I'm not going to get any information from her. I take a sip of water. Feeling the bubbles burst as they glide own my throat.

'I needed that, would you like some.' I offer the bottle to Faith.

'No thanks, I had some nectar a moment ago.'

'Are we really doing this, or am I dreaming?' I ask.

'Can a dream do this?' She asks, flying over to me and kissing the tip of my nose.'

'Yes, I think a dream could do that. That proves nothing.'

'It's happening, just accept it. I saw Smiley stop you this morning, what did he want?'

'How did you see him stop me?'

'I followed you out of town.'

'I'd appreciate you not following me, if you don't mind.'

'Just trying to keep you safe.'

'I don't need keeping safe, I can take care of myself.'

'So why did he stop you?'

'Stopped me for a faulty break light.'

'A break light, that's a bit lame. He's keeping an eye on you. You must watch him, he's after you.'

'After me? He's no reason to be, I've done nothing wrong.'

'Just be careful. I don't trust him, neither should you.'

'Why should I trust you? You're just a hallucination.'

'I'm as real as the food you're eating. Finish up, I must be going now.' Faith vanishes, taking the picnic with her.

'Hey, come back. Why do you always do that? I have a right to know what's going on, don't I?' Faith is nowhere to be seen. I'm stood in the middle of the forest, shouting to the trees. An old couple are out walking their dog. 'Good morning,' I say. Hastily they turn and walk away, ignoring me. I walk back to the car, confused. Sitting for a while to compose myself, I wonder if I'm going mad. I admit that I do feel like I've just eaten. That can't be my imagination.

Putting the key in the ignition, I turn it. The car starts on the third attempt, that's not bad going for this car. I've been driving for another two and a half hours. The "Bob Dylan" music, that's playing, fits to a 'T' the scenery I'm driving through. The roads are running well today. Before long I'm in Charmouth. I stop at a café for a cup of tea and a pasty. When the pasty arrives, I salivate. The pastry is golden brown, flaky. Juices seeping from the cracks. I pick it up with a serviette. Sinking my teeth deep, my tongue explodes with the heat. I have to spit it out, spraying the table with mashed pasty.

'Ouch!' I let it cool before I take another bite. My mind wonders again. The last time I visited Cornwall was when

Charlie and I first met. The two of us stopped in this café, all those years ago. We had a four day break at a guest house in Perranporth. I remember, we struggled getting used to each other. We were both freshly out of long-term relationships. Charlie had just got a divorce. I'd not long split up from Peter's mother. *God, I do miss you Charlie!* Why is it that the ones you love are the hardest to live with? *That's all in the past: I must start afresh.* That's the reason I left my job after seventeen years: a new start, a new beginning. I finish my tea and pasty. Feeling replenished, I leave the café. I look for a place to sit and have a smoke. Two cigarettes later, I get back in the car and continue my journey.

It's about five in the evening as I turn into Sarah's street. I pull up in the driveway, Sarah is waiting at the front door. Echoes of her youthful beauty still push through the lines that time has drawn. I notice her mouse brown hair is greying slightly and she looks a tad darker skinned. She's looking worried, then comes her beautiful smile. Sarah's smile could melt the hardest heart. We haven't see each other for nearly two years. Switching off the engine, I get out the car and rush to her.

'It's great to see you again, Sarah.' I'm exploding with emotion. 'How are you? How's Rob?'

'God, how I've missed you!' She hugs me so tightly that the bones in my back click into place. 'Are you OK, Alex? Is something up? How are the children?'

'Everything's fine,' I assure her. 'I could murder a cup of tea.'

'The kettle's on. Do you want a sandwich? Do you need to freshen up? Are you sure you're OK?' Questions,

questions, questions. They could have used her as an interrogator during the war.

'Really, I'm OK, just needed a break. James and Jay are driving me potty with all their clutter.' I walk back to the car and reach for the holdalls on the back seat.

'Can I help you with them? Is that all you've brought? Aren't you staying long? I thought you'd be here for a couple of weeks,' she says, grabbing the bags off me.

'I just picked up a few things. I didn't want to bring a lot. I'll buy some clothes whilst I'm here.' The truth is all of my clothes look like they are out of the history books, Nineties fashion. Sarah and I go into the house. Sarah's home is obsessively clean. She gets that from mum. I think back to my house, three adults trying to live in a two bed roomed terrace. James has lived with me for two and a half years; Jay has just moved in, while she waits for the contract on her new flat to complete. Jay brought all her possessions and furniture with her. Now my house looks like an auction showroom the day before a sale. Sarah and I leave the bags on the hall floor and go into the kitchen.

'What good timing, kettle's just boiled.' She pours the water into the tea pot, gives it a stir, waits just the right amount of time, then pours the tea into the cups.

'Would you like a couple of biscuits with your tea?'

'Have you got any ginger nuts?' I ask, already knowing the answer. Sarah and I have always been ginger nut addicts. Sarah puts a cup of tea and some biscuits onto the table in front of me.

'I've seen her again!' I exclaim.

'What, who? Oh no, Alex, no, not that bitch Charlie! I thought that you said that was over. She's no good for you.' Sarah's looking angry.

'No, not Charlie. I've seen the fairy again. I feel very foolish telling you this, I had to tell somebody.'

'What are you talking about, Alex? A fairy? What fairy?'

'She said she knows you.'

'Are you going off your r-rocker?' her voice tremors.

'Can you remember when we were very young? My first year at school, I think. During the school holidays, I kept getting into trouble with mum. Well, the angel is back, only she's not an angel, she's a fairy, and she's already got me into trouble again. She was following me when I was driving down. We had a picnic.'

'Alexander, stop it!' Sarah raises her voice. 'You've been under a lot of pressure lately. Maybe you should see your doctor again.'

'You have to believe me!' I protest. 'I'm not going bonkers.'

'Look, we'll talk about this later. You must be very tired after the journey. Go in to the lounge and put your feet up.'

'I'm not at all tired. When's Rob home?'

'He's had to work late again, he'll be home about seven. I phoned him at work, told him you were coming. He's looking forward to seeing you. Why don't I stick some music on. I have a great "Bob" collection.' Sarah puts on "Desire" and brings me over a foot-rest. 'There you go, put your feet up. Let me get you another cup of tea.' Fuss, fuss, fuss. Sarah would make a great mother. Sadly that does not seem to be in God's great scheme of things. Sarah and Rob have been trying for a baby for years. Yet, they've never managed. I sit listening to music and drinking my tea. I feel myself drifting into sleep to the sound of Bob's croaky tones.

"Here comes the story the hurricane. The man the
authorities came........."

When what seems like only seconds later, Sarah wakes me.
 'Alex, Alex, wake up, it's midnight.' I feel her hand
gently shake my shoulder.
 'Uh, what?' I wake up in a strange place. I'm confused.
Looking round I realise that I'm at Sarah's. She's standing
over me.
 'I think that you should go to bed now,' she says. 'Rob's
home, he didn't want to disturb you. He's gone to bed.
The bathroom's free. I'm off to bed myself. See you in the
morning.'
 'How long have I been asleep?' I lift myself off the sofa.
 'About six hours, you must have needed it, you went out
like a light. I didn't have the heart to disturb you, you
looked so peaceful,' says Sarah.
 'I'm sorry, you must think me very rude. I was looking
forward to seeing Rob again.'
 'Don't be silly; get a good night's sleep tonight, we can
spend the day together tomorrow. I've got the day off.'
I climb the stairs with legs of lead. Didn't bother to get
undressed. I just flopped out on top of the bed. Reaching
inside my holdall I grab the bottle. *Just one little night cap.*

I don't know what the time was but I was suddenly woken
by a dazzling light outside the bedroom window, a
flickering, dancing light.
 'No, not again,' I say to myself. Rushing to the window,
I pull back the curtains. Faith is sat on a branch of a giant
beech tree, waving. What does she want now?
 'Go away, I'm trying to get some sleep.'

'I just wanted to say. Don't tell Sarah about me, she won't believe you, anyway.'

'Alex, what are you doing?' Sarah has come into the room. 'You'll wake Rob.'

'Look, Sarah. She's there, in the tree.' Sarah looks out of the window. Faith has vanished again.

'There's nothing there. Go back to bed.'

'I'm sorry, sis. I must have been dreaming.' I look out the window again. All I see is the moon, shining its bright light through the leaves of the beech tree. I was beginning to question my sanity. Was the experience at home real, or had I imagined it? What about the fairy in the forest today? Was she real? I close the curtains and flop back on the bed. In no time at all, I am back into a deep sleep.

Three.

Familiar Things In Strange Places.

'It's eight o'clock, Alex,' says Sarah, peeping her head around the bedroom door. 'Have you been awake all night? Why didn't you get into bed.'

'Just a bit restless sis. Must have had too much sleep in the evening.'

'I thought we could have a walk round town today.' says Sarah, as she puts a cup of tea on the bedside table.

'It's a clear day, the forecast is good all week.' Sarah says, pulling open the curtains, and kissing me on the forehead, as she leaves the room. I love being looked after in this way. I get off the bed and take my tea downstairs. Sarah and Rob are in the dining room. I join them at the table.

'Rob! How are you? You're looking well,' I lie. He's looking older than the last time I saw him. He's aged ten years in two. Rob's always had sad looking eyes but now they look empty and tired. Rob picks up the teapot and pours himself another cup. Even his hands look old. His pitch black hair doesn't fit the rest of him.

'I'm OK, thanks Alex. How are you? How are the kids?'

'We're all OK.'

'Sarah tells me, you've come to stay for a week or two. Do you fancy a drink tonight? I can finish work early.' Rob's pleased to see me, even over enthusiastic.

'That'd be great! What are the pubs like round here?'

'The White Heart's not bad, not too busy. We can have a good chat. They've got real ale, you still a fan?'

'I do like it but tend not to drink it much these days. It's much stronger than the beer I drink.'

'I remember a time when you and your friend Mike, would drink nothing else. You were both connoisseurs.'

'I'm a bit of a light weight now, can't drink much at all.' Sarah looks at me knowingly. She must have seen the vodka bottle in my bag.

'I'm off to work shortly,' says Rob. 'I'll be back about five. We can catch up a bit later.'

'Ok, Rob, that sounds great! Don't work too hard. See you later.'

After breakfast, Sarah and I drive into the town. We spend the morning walking round the local shopping centre. I'm weighed down with several bags of new clothes.

'Fancy something to eat?' I ask.

'That's a good idea,' says Sarah. 'My friend owns a tea-house just off the High Street. She's single,' Sarah emphasises.

'I just want some thing to eat, I'm not looking for a date.'

Sarah thinks that I need a woman. She's scared that if I don't find one soon, I'll get back with Charlie. Charlie, was the love of my life. But the seven year relationship was a no go from the start. Not too many of my friends or family approved of her, they did not know her like I did. Without Charlie, I would not be where I am today. Wherever that may be.

'Here we are.' Sarah, interrupts my thoughts. We're standing outside a quaint-looking tea house. The usual paper doilies and gingham table cloths. As we step across the threshold, a strange feeling sweeps through me, a feeling of de-ja vu. There are only three other customers in the place: an old man dressed in brown corduroy trousers and tweed jacket and a young couple dressed in high street fashion. They are chatting and laughing, enjoying each others company. The sweet aroma of fresh baked cakes fills the air. I become aware of a strikingly beautiful woman behind the counter. She is a little shorter than me. Her hair is golden blond, shoulder length with loose curls. Her eyes, a piercing blue. She is staring straight at me, as if she knows me. Sarah walks up to her. They kiss each other on the cheek.

'Faye, this is my brother, Alex. Alex, this is Faye.'

'What? Who?' I walk up to Faye and shake her hand. As I do, a static shock passes between the two of us. I snatch my hand away quickly.

'Wow! That stung,' I say, shaking my hand.

'That happens all the time. Something to do with static,' says Faye.

'I have a friend, who has the same problem.' I say. I find myself staring. I am transfixed by her looks, her lips, her skin of alabaster. There's something different about this woman. I can't put my finger on it, she radiates an aura, a glow. I'm smitten, I almost swoon. Sarah, nudges me. She whispers.

'Alex, stop staring.'

'Two cream teas, please,' I blurt.

'Yes, it's nice to meet you, too,' replies Faye, looking at me oddly. I feel stupid. I am acting like a twelve year old who's only just discovered the opposite sex. Sarah drags me towards a table and sits me down.

'What was that all about? You're acting very strange, Alex,' Sarah starts her questioning again. 'Have you not met a woman lately? First, you stare at Faye as if she's from Mars, then you demand two cream teas like a mad man.'

'I'm sorry, Sarah, she's very pretty. I just felt a bit self-conscious. I look like crap. All I ever wear is these jeans an tee-shirt. I'm afraid that I haven't made a good impression.' Sarah looks at me in disbelief.

'Five minutes ago you said that you weren't looking for a date,' she laughs. 'Now, you look like you'd move heaven and earth to spend some time with Faye.'

'Do you think she might be interested in me?

'Oh, I don't know Alex. You've only just met her.' Faye brings the cream teas over to our table.

'Enjoy!' she says, with a smile. Steam rises from the teapot spout, the scones are large with a generous helping of cream and strawberries. They look as good as a photograph in a recipe book, the way real food never looks. I feel my mouth watering.

'Are you staying long, Alex?' asks Faye.

'No, I have to meet Rob for a drink later.' Faye's, eyebrows furrow, with puzzlement.

'I mean are you staying with Sarah, long?'

'Oh, I'm sorry,' I say. 'I'll be staying about two weeks. If Sarah can put up with me.'

'Don't be silly, Alex. You can stay as long as you want.' Faye walks back to serve another customer.

'Alex, just relax; you're dribbling!'

'I'm just not used to talking to women anymore. I'm out of practice.'

'How are Jay and the boys?' asks Sarah, changing the subject. 'I bet they're getting quite grown up.'

'You could say that. Jay was twenty two last month, James is twenty and Peter's fourteen. They don't stay children for long. Jay is buying her own flat. That's why she's staying with me at the moment, just waiting for contracts to exchange.'

'You're joking, Jay buying a flat! It seems only yesterday, she was at school.'

'Yes, it all makes me feel very old. James is starting at the Metropolitan University in September, Film studies. Even Peter has a paper round. My babies have all grown up. What about you Sarah, how are you? Are you still happy living down here?'

'I love it here, it's so peaceful, Rob is less stressed. No more commuting back and forth to the office. The only thing that could make us happier is a baby,' Sarah's face takes on a sad look. 'You're so fortunate to have three such fantastic children.' I look at Sarah.

'I know, I wouldn't swap them for the world.'

'How's Mum?' Sarah enquires. 'I haven't spoken to her this week.'

'Still running 'round like she's twenty.'

'It's good that she keeps herself occupied.'

'Yea, she's always on the go since Dad died. She spends a lot of her time with friends from the art group.'

'Do you remember her always pushing us to paint?'

'She pushed you more. She gave up with me. I would make a mess on purpose. That stopped her trying.'

'It's strange,' Sarah says. 'But I feel more like getting out the old paint brushes, these days. Something to fill my time.'

'Why do you need to fill time? I thought You and Rob kept busy.'

'We used to. It's just, Rob has to work late a lot know.'

'Rob, always hated working, more than was needed. Your not short of money are you?'

'No, it's not money. They have a lot of important new contracts.' We finish our cream teas, I mop my mouth, fold the napkin, rest it on the plate and get up to leave.

'You off now?' asks Faye. 'I'll ring you tonight, Sarah. Bye, Alex. I hope you enjoy your stay.'

Sarah and I say "bye" to Faye. I walk through the doorway. As I do, my foot catches on the step, sending me head-first into the path of a passing pedestrian.

'I'm so very sorry,' I say.

'Steady on pal, are you drunk?'

'Of course I'm not drunk, pal. Just tripped on the step.'

'You should try and be a bit more careful and watch where you're going.'

'I said "sorry", didn't I. As I look up at the stranger, I instantly recognise him. It's Smiley, the policeman. He's not in uniform but I'd recognise that red hair and silly smug grin, anywhere. My blood boils.

'You again! What are you doing? Are you following me?'

'What's your problem, I'd keep away from the booze if I were you,' says Smiley.

'I think we'd better get you home,' says Sarah, grabbing me by the arm and pulling me away.

'Sorry John,' She says to Smiley. Then turns to me. 'You don't seem to be coping very well today.'

'It's the policeman from yesterday morning. He must have followed me down here.'

'What policeman?'

'Him, the one I just bumped into.'

'No, that's John, he's not a policeman.' says Sarah. 'He owns the local fruit and veg shop. Let's get you home.'

Four.

Paranoia.

It's seven thirty in the evening. Sarah, Rob and I are sitting down, eating our dinner. Rob has prepared a succulent roast lamb, with potatoes, steamed vegetables and a rich gravy. The lamb melts as I chew. The broccoli, carrots and cauliflower are crisp, the potatoes are fluffy and the gravy is smooth, rich deep brown and complements the lamb.

'You really do know how to cook Rob. I haven't had a meal this tasty in years.'

'Don't tell him that, you'll not be able to get his head through the door.'

'People have said that about my cooking skills before,' says Rob, with pride.

'Your cooking was always Ok, Alex. You certainly don't look like you starve!' says Sarah with a giggle, patting me on my tummy.

'That's junk food for you. Ten minutes in the microwave from frozen.'

'You don't use them, do you? You were always against ready meals. You called it "lazy food."'

'Yes, I know, I'm a hypocrite.' After our meal, Rob and I clear away the dinner things and wash up. Sarah is on the phone to one of her friends.

'Ready for a drink?' Rob asks. 'How about you Sarah, are you sure you don't want to come?'

'No, you go, I've some paper work that I want to catch up with. I think I can cope with missing out on you two talking nonsense after you've had a few drinks.' Rob and I get ready to leave for the pub.

'See you later sweetie,' Rob says, pecking Sarah on the cheek.

'Ok sweetie. Alex, no leading him astray, I want him back in one piece.'

'I promise that I'll be good,' I say. 'See you later, sis.' We take a gentle stroll to the pub, catching up on old times, on the way.

'Have you seen Charlie lately?' Rob asks.

'See her every now an then.'

'She was gorgeous, don't know why you split up.'

'We would have ended up killing each other.'

'S'pose you still having the time of your life. A different woman every week.'

'I wish I was. Can't seem to find the right woman anymore. They're all too tame after Charlie.'

'I thought sport fucking was your hobby.'

'Tell you what Rob, I can't even get it up. Don't know if it's the tablets or I'm just past it.'

'What tablets? What d'ya take tablets for?'

'Antidepressants', don't tell Sarah. You know what she's like. She'll only worry.'

'You don't seem depressed, how long you been on them?'

'Couple of years now. Not long after Charlie and me split up.'

'And they stop your dick working, do they?'

'Don't know if it's the tablets or my state of mind. But I ain't had a decent stiffy for bloody ages.'

'Never thought I'd hear you say that.'

'I know, I've tried loads of women since Charlie. I'm getting tired of showing so many of them what a crap lover I am. So I don't bother anymore.' As we near the pub. I change the conversation.

'What's this pub like?'

'It's Ok. Tony, the landlord keeps a good pint. And it's handy, not too far to stagger home,' Rob jokes. As we enter the pub, the landlord greets Rob.

'Usual, Rob?'

'Make it two, is that Ok, Alex? 'Six X', good stuff.'

'Fine by me. Haven't had a good drink in a long time.' We find a quiet corner. As soon as we sit, Rob starts to speak.

'Alex, Sarah and me, we're going through a bit of a bad time at the moment.'

'What? You always seem so happy.'

'We still love each other very much,' Rob assures me. 'It's this baby thing. The doctors say that Sarah can't have children. She feels that she's depriving me.

'What? It's no one's fault.'

'I know that. She gets really tearful at times. At first I could cope but the longer it's gone on, the harder I find it.'

'Come on Rob, stick with her. You need to support each

other through this.'

'I can't convince her that I don't mind as long as I have her, she's enough for me. I am working long hours, just to avoid being home in the evenings.'

'How is working long hours going to convince her you love her? Sarah thinks you've just got a lot of extra work on. Seems to me, your avoiding the problem.'

'Her sadness is bringing me down. All I want is for her to believe me.' Rob's face is scarlet, I've never seen him look so worried.

'What about adoption?' I ask.

'I've suggested adoption. She says "It's not the same as having our own child." Sarah thinks I should find someone else, someone who can give me children.'

'I didn't know things were so bad.'

'Would you talk to Sarah for me? I love her so much, I don't want to lose her,' Rob pleads. 'She'll listen to you. You two have always been very close.' Rob is near to tears as he talks to me. He's struggling to keep it together. I wonder how long this has all been bottled up.

'Of course I'll talk with her. Sarah wouldn't be able to cope without you. I think she must be feeling guilty because she knows how much you want children.'

'I did want children. I wanted children with Sarah. As long as I have her, that's what's really important to me. She just can't seem to accept that.'

'Please, don't worry Rob,' I try to reassure him. 'I will talk to her tomorrow. Things have a way of working out in the end.'

'I hope so,' says Rob. As we down our pints. 'Same again,' he asks, as he stands.

'I'll get these,' I gesture him to sit. Taking the glasses to the bar.

'Two pints of "Six X" please.'

'Anything else?' asks the landlord.

'No thanks.' I turn and look around the bar whilst I wait for the drinks. In the far corner, I spot Smiley. My heart misses a beat. His chair is facing towards the table that Rob and I are sat at. He is Smiley. I'm sure it's him. He is following me!

'Three pounds ninety, please, sir... Sir that comes to three pounds ninety.' There's a tap on my shoulder. It's the landlord. 'Three pounds and ninety pence,' he says.

'Sorry, I was miles away.' Still looking at Smiley, I take a fiver out of my pocket and hand it over. Picking up the drinks, I walk back to our table.

'Rob, that chap down the other end of the bar, the tall one, is he a policeman?'

'Who, John? No, he's the local grocer, nice bloke. Captain of the darts team.'

'It's just that he looks like a policeman that I had a run-in with yesterday morning.

'You, a run-in with the police? I don't believe it! What've you been up to?'

'Oh, it was nothing, a case of mistaken identity. It's just that I have seen him twice today and I thought that he might be following me. I'm sounding paranoid, aren't I!'

'Just a bit. Relax, enjoy your drink, I can assure you that John is not a policeman. He took over the grocer shop about ten years ago.' We both down our second beer.

'That's a good pint. Tony really does know how to keep a good beer,' says Rob.

'Yes, it is good,' I mutter, with my eye still on the Smiley look-alike. I try to put my fears to the back of my mind. So many strange things have happened to me today.

Something is not quite right. First, Faye looks at me as if she knows me, then I am sure John is PC Smiley. When Rob gets up to get another drink. I overhear him talking to the landlord.

'Same again please, Tony,' Rob says. 'Oh, and two whisky chasers.'

'You two on a bender tonight?.

'No, just not had a drink in a while' Rob laughs.

'The bloke you're with, is he Ok?' Tony enquires. 'He seems a bit strange, I don't want any trouble.'

'You won't get any trouble from him. The only trouble he gets into, is women trouble.'

'Oh, he forgot his change earlier,' says Tony, handing Rob my change. Rob re-joins me at the table.

'I am glad you've come to stay,' Rob says, putting the beer and whisky on the table, spilling some.

'I can't drink all that!' I protest. 'I'll be able to manage the beer, I'm not too good with whisky.'

'Come on, get it down you, it'll keep the cold out, on the walk home.' I manage to drink up. The whisky goes straight to my head. I look up, John has come over to our table.

'Hi Rob. What you doing down here tonight? The missus let you out?'

'Just popped in for a drink and a chat. This is my brother in law, Alex. Alex this is John.'

'We've already met, Sarah introduced us earlier,' says John.

'Yes, we bumped into each other at the tea house.' I say.

'Do you fancy a game of darts?' asks John. 'Me and Mark against you two?

'Yes, sure, is that alright?' Rob asks me.

'I haven't played in years but I'm up for it. Just point me in the right direction.'

Rob introduces me to Mark, John's friend. Mark has one of those chubby, cheeky, likeable faces. It's ruddy from drink. His cheeks look like two big red apples. As I get to my feet to shake his hand, I stumble a little.

'Are you Ok?' Rob asks, grabbing hold of my arm to steady me.

'Yes. Just stood up a bit too quick, got a head rush. Another beer will put that right.' I get some more drinks in while John, Mark and Rob clear a few chairs away from the dart board area. I feel a bit uneasy with John. The landlord puts the drinks on a tray. I didn't realise how drunk I was, until I lift the tray and turn to walk to the others. I spill a bit of beer with every step. At this rate we'll be drinking halves! The beer sloshes over the edges of the glasses. Finally, after what seems an age, I get to the table. It's a relief to put the tray down.

'We're going to need a ladder to get down into those drinks,' John jokes.

'Sorry about that.'

'What are we playing? Three-o-one? Do you two know how to play?' asks Mark.

'Yeah. We can play that with our eyes closed,' says Rob.

'You'll think that I have got my eyes closed, when you see me play.' I say, with a drunken grin.

'Closest to the bull throws first,' says John. I pick up the vibe that John takes his darts seriously. I think perhaps he'll not enjoy playing against me as I find it hard to take anything seriously when I've had a few drinks.

'So, Alex, what brings you down to our neck of the woods?' John enquires.

'I just thought that I would have a change of scenery. I haven't seen Rob and Sarah for a while.'

'We're starting, John,' Mark interrupts.

'Right, here we go then. Double tops to start, I think.' Before John has finished the statement, his first dart is sitting in the double twenty. His next two, bed themselves deep into the triple twenty. Well, I hope Rob is good at darts, otherwise this game is going to be a whitewash.

'You can throw first, Alex,' says Rob. 'The dart board is the round thing with the wire mesh stuck to the front and the darts go pointy end first.'

'Mock no more, let the games begin.' I stand ready, take aim. My first dart glides swiftly from my hand and lands dead centre of the double twenty.

'Looks like we have a game on our hands, Mark,' says John. My first shot was a fluke. I steady myself for the next throw. I'm concentrating my aim, looking at the triple twenty. The second dart leaves my grip, hits the wire, then plummets to the floor.

'Bad luck, old chap,' Mark chips in and shoots a glance towards John. They smile to each other. I must save face with this dart. Again, I take aim and throw. Thud. This time the dart buries itself into the wooden surround of the dart board.

'Oops, it takes me a while to warm up,' I say, trying to hide my embarrassment. I make way for Mark to take his place in front of the board, walk over to the table, I pick up my beer. John is sipping his beer and watching Mark.

'Have you got any family in Southampton?' I ask John.

'No, my family are all west country folk.'

'It's just that you look familiar, you sure we haven't met?'

'Only today, when you tried knocking me into the road.'

'Yea, sorry about that.'

'What do you do for a living?' John asks.

'Nothing at the moment. I've taken a year out, to change direction. I got fed up working for other people, so I thought that I would give it a try on my own.'

'So you're on the dole then. It's alright for some.' John's tone is not at all friendly.

'No, I'm living off the money that I got from my old employer. They paid me off with a sum large enough to last a year. Not that there's anything wrong with being on the dole for a short while, if a person needs it.'

'Oh, so you got a golden handshake. I can't afford to take time off, as I run my own shop.'

'Well, what I intend to do, is work for myself. It's just a matter of finding a hole in the market and trying to fill it.'

'Are you two ladies paying attention?' Rob calls across. 'Your throw, John.'

'Who's winning?' I ask Rob, as if I didn't know the answer.

'They are in the lead, even after your hefty score of forty. I didn't expect to win anyway, these two are in the darts team, they play all the time,' Rob laughs. 'You're swaying. Have you had too much to drink?'

'No. I've only just got started. Who's round is it, anyway?'

'I'll get these. John, Mark, another pint?' Rob holds up his glass and shakes it at the others.

'Stick a whisky on the side, Rob,' says Mark.

'Do you two want a chaser?' Rob asks John and me.

'Go on then,' replies John. I decline a chaser, I can still feel the effects of the earlier one. Whisky just does not agree with me anymore. It's my throw again. I have no clue what the score is. I don't even know what I'm supposed to be aiming for. I don't even care. I am aware that the others are chuckling at my technique. This time all three darts land in the board. I couldn't say whereabouts. Rob has come back with the drinks. As he puts the glasses down, he clears away the empties and returns them to the bar. John starts his questions again. I don't like talking to him but I'm polite for Rob's sake.

'Are you married Alex? Do you have any children?'

'No, I'm divorced. I have three children. How about you?'

'No, I've never been married, just waiting for the right woman to come along.'

'I think that the right woman for me has just come along. My sister has this great looking friend, Faye. The woman who runs the tea-house, in the High Street. I'm hoping that I can pluck up courage to ask her out while I'm down here.' John's face takes on a look of anger.

'You don't stand a chance with her. I don't think she likes men, if you know what I mean, rug muncher. I've asked her out before. She's just not interested. I think I have the wrong equipment for her needs!'

'Well, there's no harm in trying,' I say. 'She seemed friendly enough earlier today when Sarah and I went in for a bite to eat.'

'It's up to you mate but I'm telling you, you're wasting your time.' John's voice is unfriendly. Looks like I might be stepping on someone's toes. So what if I am? This bloke's a caveman.

'Yeees!' a cheer bellows out from Mark. 'The undefeatable go undefeated!' I can't help thinking to myself that these two need something more in their lives.

'Fancy another game, lads?' Mark asks.

'No, must be off,' says John. 'I have an early start. Some of us have to keep the country going. Been nice to meet you, Alex.' John holds out his hand to shake mine. I return the gesture. He studies my face deeply as we shake. Mark picks his jacket off the back of a chair.

'See you later lads. Thanks for the game,' says Mark. John gives me a steely look as he leaves. I think that I've made an enemy tonight.

'Are you ready to go then? I think we've both had enough to drink,' says Rob.

'What's his problem?' I ask Rob. 'He's not very friendly, is he?'

'I don't know. He's usually Ok: must have just had a bad day.' We say our goodbyes to the landlord and we make our way out into the chill air. The two of us stumble our way home.

'I meant what I said, Alex,' says Rob. 'I'm glad that you have come to stay. I know that Sarah is really pleased to see you again; she's been worried about you since you and Charlie split up.'

'I'm Ok. I do miss Charlie. I know that we couldn't go on, too hectic together. It was driving us mad.'

'I can't believe your not seeing anyone else?'

'I told you, I've not been looking. Just wanted some time to myself and the children,' I say. 'Mind you, I met one of Sarah's friends today, her name is Faye. Do you know her?'

'Faye, the fairy cake lady,' Rob announces. 'Yes I know her. I'm not sure she's right for you though. She's really nice but she's into all that mystic stuff, aromatherapy and tarot cards. You know the type, always looking for something that's not there.'

'The fairy cake lady?'

'Yes, her cakes contain that little something extra, makes you think that you can fly!' Rob laughs. 'Sarah and I had some when we first met her. I've never seen Sarah so relaxed and so full of laughter.' Suddenly, Faith whizzes by, flying between the trees.

'I told you to leave me alone!' I shout.

'What,' asks Rob.

'I was talking to her,' I point to the trees.

'Who?'

'Her. Can't you see her?'

'You've had too much to drink.'

'Look in the tree, don't tell me you can't see her. She's been following me for days.'

'There's no-one in the tree. Come on lets get home and have a coffee.' I resign myself to the fact that Faith won't show herself to anyone else. The walk home takes no time at all. Sarah's standing, looking out of the window. As we get to the house, she opens the door.

'Shush you two,' she says, putting her finger to her lips. 'I could hear you coming from the other end of the road. Get inside before you wake the neighbours.' Rob and I slump on the sofa. Sarah brings us coffee.

'You'd think that a couple of teenagers were walking down the road, the noise you were making.' She is still smiling. 'You'd better drink your coffee and sober up a bit. Oh Alex, I had a phone call this evening, from Faye. She was asking a lot about you. I think you should ask her out one night this week but don't tell her I said so.'

'Two little love birds,' Rob pipes up. 'Alex has been asking about her as well. Must be love at first sight.'

'You could do with a night out with a nice woman,' says Sarah.

'You'd get on well with her, if you relax a bit and stop stumbling over your words and feet when she's around.'

I want to have this conversation about Faye but the drink has gone to my head. I decide to go to bed. Sitting on the bed, I think about Faith. Why does she keep pestering me? Slumping over, I drift into sleep, my head filled with visions of Faye.

Five.

The Chase.

When I wake in the morning, I feel great. I haven't felt this good in a long time. My bladder is full to bursting. I have to run to the toilet and only just get the lid up in time. After a quick freshen up, I go down stairs to be greeted by an empty house. There is a note on the dining room table. It's from Sarah.

"Alex, we have gone off to work, make yourself at home. Have a great day. See you when I get back, about 4:30. Love Sarah." I look at my watch. It's 11:15: I've not slept this late in ages. I always wake myself up with a coffee and a fag; I go into the garden. Sarah and Rob don't smoke, so it's only fair not to stink the house out. The sun is already high in the sky. It feels good to know that I don't have to go to work. Leaving that job was the best thing I have ever done.

Looking around the garden, I think that Sarah is turning into our mother. The garden is full of flowers. Sarah's garden is about three times the size of mine. It must take a lot of looking after. As work is Rob's way of retreating from their problems, I guess that the garden is Sarah's way of escaping. There are two cabbage white butterflies dancing with each other. They instantly bring to mind Faith. *She had better leave me alone today.*

I wonder how things are back home. I go back inside the house and decide to phone straight away. The telephone has hardly a chance to ring before it's picked up.

'Yellow,' says the voice.

'James, it's Dad, how are you ? Is everything alright?'

'Hi Dad, yes, everything's fine.'

'Did Peter come round to feed the cat and chickens, yesterday?'

'Yes, he came after his paper-round. When are you coming home? Peter's been asking if I know.'

'I'm not sure yet, maybe another week or so. I'll let you know closer to the time.'

'How are aunt Sarah and uncle Rob?'

'They're both well. You should see the house and garden down here, they're stunning. You should bring Kate down sometime.'

'Yeh, maybe in the Summer.'

'Don't forget to eat properly. I don't want you living off junk food.'

'No, I'll be eating well. Kate has come to stay. We're going to take turns to cook the evening meal.'

'That sounds good. Perhaps you could keep up the cooking skills when I get home! I better let you get on; I'm

49

sure you think I worry too much. Say 'hello' to Jay and Peter for me. Tell them I'll not be gone too much longer. See you later.'

'OK, Dad, see you soon.' The phone goes dead. I really miss my children. I keep forgetting they're old enough to take care of themselves. Why do I still worry about them?

What to do with myself today? A thought enters my head. *Should I go to the tea-house? Would I be able to act like a human being if I saw Faye?*

'Yes, go on. Go and see Faye.' Faith has appeared again.

'Can't I just have one day without you popping by?'

'Only trying to help. Go on, dress up smart and give her a visit.'

'Why is it so important to you, what I do?'

'I just think the two of you would do each other some good.'

'Do you know Faye as well? Do you keep hassling her?'

'You're not very kind to me Alex. I get the impression you don't like me.'

'It's not that I don't like you. But I should have stopped having imaginary friends years ago.'

'I keep telling you, I am real.' With that Faith flies over and pinches my arm.'

'Ow! You bitch. That hurt.'

'See, that's real enough.' I look down and see a bright red mark on my arm.

'Alex, don't you think John looks a lot like Smiley?'

'Yes I do. Thought it was him at first. Rob and Sarah say that he's lived down here for years.'

'Well just keep your eye on him, I don't trust him either.'

'God, you're just as paranoid as me.'

'Just want you to be careful around him. Anyway, that's enough about him. You go and get dressed in the smart stuff you got yesterday. Go and see Faye.'

'You're bossy for a little one aren't you.' Taking Faith's advice, I go back in the house. After a quick shower, I dress in the smartest casual clothes that I purchased yesterday. Black shoes, cream chinos and a black shirt, topped off with sun glasses and my best watch. Faith is still in the garden when I get back down.

'Well, how do I look?'

'Good, you look good.'

'Can't believe I'm asking "Tinkerbell" for fashion tips.'

'Well you needed to ask someone, your dress sense has been pretty shoddy lately.'

'You don't believe in pulling punches, do you?'

'Off you go then, I'm sure Faye will be pleased to see you.'

'You're not going to tag along, are you?'

'Don't worry, I'll leave you to your own devices. See you around handsome.' With that Faith vanishes.

It doesn't take me long to drive to the shopping centre. My stomach's in knots. I can feel myself getting anxious as I near Faye's tea house. *Why am I so nervous lately? I used to be full of confidence. Did all the years with Charlie really take away all my zest, my confidence, my love of life? There it is, the tea-shop. I'll just have a cigarette before I go in.* I take the smoke deep into my lungs. *Yes, that's good, nothing like a smoke to calm the nerves. What if Faye doesn't smoke? She'll smell it on me: that'd put her off straight away. I wonder if there's a shop nearby that sells gum?* I stub my cigarette out, luckily just around the corner is a newsagents. I buy some gum, into my mouth go two strips. I chomp down. *Right, deep breath. Here I go, destiny awaits.* Through the door of the tea-house I go. Ring, ring, ring. A bell attached to the door announces my arrival. I didn't notice the bell yesterday. The place is a lot busier today. Some of the customers turn to see who's entered. I start to feel very self-conscious again. *Am I walking normally? Do I look alright? Have I got two heads?* The seconds it takes to walk to the counter seem like hours. Everything's moving in slow motion. I'm breathing deeply to calm myself. *Be cool, take your time, don't speak like a lunatic,* I say to myself. I reach the counter, behind which Faye is standing.

'Hello, remember me?' I ask, trying to sound full of confidence. Faye smiles.

'Yes, I remember you, you're the chap who attacked one of my customers as you were leaving yesterday.'

'Yes, that's my way of meeting people. I find shaking hands a shocking experience just lately.'

'What can I get you?' Faye asks.

'Pot of tea an a carrot cake, please.'

'Take a seat. I'll bring it over,' she says with a enchanting smile. Faye is truly a stunning woman. Could I really expect to have a chance of taking her out? After a short while, Faye brings over my tea. She sits down, facing me.

'Feels good to take the weight off my feet!' she exclaims. 'You don't mind me sitting down for a while, do you?'

'No, you sit there as long as you like, I'm glad of the company. It's been a while since I've had the chance to talk to a pretty woman.' Faye blushes. *Am I going too fast? Have I forgotten how to flirt without sounding smarmy?*

'Why, thank you, kind sir, I think you flatter me.'

Is she fishing for compliments? When did I forget how to play the chasing game?

'I'm sure you must get flattered all the time,' I say. Her eyes are the bluest, blue I've ever seen. They seem to be able to see deep into my soul.

'God! I would love to drink the sweet nectar of your kiss.'

'What?' Asks Faye, looking shocked. *Oh no, I said that out loud.*

'I should have worn a neck tie with this.'

'Yes, if you say so,' replies Faye, looking at me, puzzled.

'Excuse me, Miss,' a voice from behind me calls. Faye is taken away from me in the nick of time, before I have the chance to say anything else wrong. I'm a fool. I know she finds me attractive but I'm going to blow it if I carry on like this. I must pluck up the courage to ask her out to dinner. *Just be polite, don't say anything silly, don't stutter. I'll wait for the right moment, let her be free from customers. Then, if she says "no", nobody can witness her rejection of me.* Faye returns to my table, once she's finished with the other customer.

'Alex, would you like to take me out tomorrow night?' She asks. *Wow! Problem solved!* I couldn't believe my luck. I have a date with the woman of my dreams. I didn't even have to ask.

'Yes please! I mean, yes, yes it would be my pleasure.' That sounded desperate.

'Here's my phone number, give me a call tonight about eight, that gives me time to get home from work.' Faye hands me her phone number on a little card; the card is covered in glitter. Rob told me she's a bit airy-fairy.'

'Alex, did you get dressed in the dark this morning?' Faye asks.

'No, why do you say that? I thought I looked quite smart today.'

'You do, all except for the socks,' she says. I look down towards my feet. My trouser legs have ridden up, revealed beneath them is one black sock and one brown. I kick myself mentally. How did that happen? I don't even own brown socks. I am sure that they were both black when I put them on this morning.

'Oops, that's my other way of getting noticed,' I say, trying to hide my embarrassment. I tuck into the cake with gusto.

'You seem a little hungry.'

'Yes. I've not eaten since last night.'

'Ooh, last night, that's such a long time ago. I bet you'd last five minutes on a desert island.' Faye picks up a napkin and mops some cream from my chin. I feel embarrassed again; I joke to hide my blushing.

'Mum's starting me on solids soon. I may be allowed to use a knife and fork!'

'You're just a little bit silly, aren't you?' Faye has a coy grin on her face. I think maybe she could be just a little silly too. It makes a nice change to meet a woman who does not take herself too seriously. I'm going to have to watch my step. I always fall too quickly for women like her. As I finish the cake, Faye teases me.

'That's got to be a record! I've never seen a cake disappear so quickly. Wait here a moment, I'm just going to get the "Guinness Book of Records" on the phone.'

'I'll be gone before they get here.'

'I hope you don't do everything at the speed of light,' she says with a cheeky, flirtatious look. Did she just imply what I hoped she implied? Or am I reading the signs wrong again?

'I slow down in the evenings. I've even been mistaken for dead at times.'

'If that happens, I'll just have to give you the kiss of life.'

I know that I didn't miss-read that. I get an excited knot in my stomach, I know I'm going to start talking gibberish if I don't leave soon. Best leave whilst the going's good. I make my excuses. I look at my watch and pretend I've arranged to meet Rob.

'I didn't realise the time, I must go. I told Rob I'd visit his works this afternoon. I'll see you tomorrow Faye,' I'm just about to leave when Faye leans over and kisses me, lightly, on the cheek. She static shocks me again.

'See you tomorrow,' she says. 'Don't forget to phone me tonight.'

'I won't forget, and I'll even try to put on matching socks tomorrow.'

'Alex,' Faye calls after me.

'Yes?'

'Watch your step on the way out!'

Six.

Mixed Emotions.

I feel great, I'm dancing all the way back to Rob and Sarah's house, only in my mind. Don't want any more funny looks.

'Faye and Alex sitting up a tree K, I, S, S, I, N, G.' Faith is flying just above my head, singing a childish song. 'She pretty isn't she?' I am no longer shocked by Faith's sudden appearances. I suppose you can get used to anything if it happens often enough.

'What do you want now? Have you nothing better to do with your time, other than follow me around?'

'Just thought I'd see how my favourite human is doing. So what do you think of Faye? Is she your type?'

'You tell me, you seem to know everything about me.'

'She's perfect, not too nutty, like some of your others.'

'What's wrong with nutty? I'm talking to you in broad daylight. Don't you think that's nutty?'

'I don't but they do,' says Faith, pointing to a couple who have stopped still and staring at me talking to myself.

'I'm going to stop talking to you now, before I'm put in the loony bin.' With that I march off down the street.

'You can't get away from me that easily!' Shouts Faith, flying after me. 'I might even come on your date with you tomorrow night.' Then she disappears again. I'm really looking forward to going out with Faye tomorrow night but if Faith turns up she'll ruin everything.

'Please, please leave us alone tomorrow night.' I call out.

It's been a while since I've had a proper date. I can feel the excitement building. I can't wait to tell Sarah and Rob. When I get to the house, I realise I didn't pick up the front door key. It's only 2:30. Sarah won't be back for some time yet. I'll just have to wait in the back garden. I'm dying for a pee. I look around for somewhere to go. Behind the garden shed, that's a good place. I'm standing happily peeing behind the shed, up against the fence.

'Good afternoon.' I turn, startled but can see nobody, when all of a sudden up pops Sarah's neighbour, just the other side of the fence. He's not noticed what I'm doing. He is a tall man. Looks like "Captain Birds Eye" looked in the adverts of my early years. White hair, bushy white eyebrows. He has a sympathetic face.

'Oh, hello,' I say, trying to act normally. 'Sorry for the intrusion, I was just looking at your garden. Sarah said that it was beautiful. She's right.' All this time I'm still peeing: once I've started, I just can't stop.

'Thank you,' he says. 'Fred Spelling.' He reaches his

hand over the fence to shake mine. I have to let go of myself to return the gesture. His grip is firm, I can feel the calluses on his hands.

'Pleased to meet you. I'm Alex, Sarah's brother.' We shake hands. I'm getting more uncomfortable as pee is running down my trouser leg. I do hope that he doesn't want to talk for long.

'Yes, Sarah said, this morning, that you'd come to stay.'

'I've locked myself out. So I thought I'd have a look around the gardens, they're all very nice around here.'

'Locked out eh, that's no good. Why don't you pop over for a cup of tea?' *Why, oh why did I have to mention that I was locked out?*

'Thank you, no, I'd hate to intrude.'

'Nonsense man, it'll be no intrusion, I insist. Don't bother walking round, just hop over the low part in the fence.' As I turn to walk down the garden, I quickly put myself away. Reaching the low section in the fence, I spring over it like a young gazelle. Only to catch my foot on the fence and land flat on my face. Up I jump.

'Are you OK?' Fred asks. His eyes scanning me from top to toe, they stop on the wet patch.

'I'm fine, nothing a few weeks in hospital won't sort out.' I lie about the wet patch on my trousers. 'Had an accident at the tea house today, dropped the cup on my lap.'

'Just doesn't seem to be your day,' he mumbles distractedly. I think he's beginning to wish he hadn't invited me over. I know I am.

'You must spend a lot of time working in the garden. It looks fantastic.'

'Keeps me active, it used to be a jungle. When I retired from the Merchant Navy, I felt I was going round the bend with nothing to occupy myself. That's when I took up gardening. It's been a life saver.'

'Well, you could certainly show some of those gardeners on the TV makeover programs a few things.'

'They've only got a few days, I've been working on this for over ten years now. It takes the first eight years for the garden to establish. Now the hard work's done, it's just a case of keeping on top of things and keeping it tidy.'

'I've only got a very simple garden, a lawn with a few bushes and trees. It's a low maintenance, great for lazy summer days.'

'Gardening is for the retired,' Fred replies. 'It's hard to do a week's work then spend your days off working in the garden.'

'That's exactly how I feel, weekends for rest and leisure. How long were you at sea for?'

'Too many years to count. I boarded my first ship at the age of fourteen and spent the whole of my working life travelling the world on many ships. I grew my land legs back just after my sixty first birthday.'

'That must have been great. I bet you've seen most of the world. Most people don't even see their own country.'

'The only thing with being in the Merchant Navy for all those years is that you never feel you have a home. I bought this place over forty years ago. It was just a base, somewhere to sleep when on leave. Only started to feel like home after I left the sea.'

'Is there a Mrs Spelling?'

'No; there nearly was many years ago but that's a different story.'

'I'm sorry, I didn't mean to pry.'

'No, that's Ok. I once had the most wonderful woman in

the world, we were deeply in love. I was going to give up life at sea so we could be together. We talked of marriage and children. Then, one day she left, I never even had a chance to kiss her goodbye. I was knocked for six after Sophie left. I could see no future for myself other than on ships. I never met another like her.' I could see the hurt in Fred's face. Thought I'd better change the subject.

'What are house prices like in this area? I'm toying with selling up and moving down this way.'

'To tell you the truth, I haven't a clue. I've never given a thought to moving since I bought the place.'

'I can't imagine they will be as cheap as they are back home. You have so much land around you.'

We spend the afternoon with Fred showing me round his garden. Explaining all the types of flowers and plants. Lots of stories from Fred's days at sea. After about two hours, I start to get a little bored. Looking at my watch, I say.

'Goodness, it's 4:30 already. Sarah will be thinking I've got lost, she's such a worrier, she'll be sending out a search party.'

'Yes, I must be thinking what to get for dinner tonight,' says Fred.

'Well, thank you for a pleasant afternoon Fred. It's been a pleasure meeting you.'

'Anytime you're at a loss or lock yourself out, just come on round,' Fred says. 'I don't get out too much nowadays.'

'I'll hold you to that. See you again, bye.'

'Bye, Alex.' This time, when I get to the fence, I climb over it very carefully.

Sarah and Rob are home from work and in the kitchen.

I enter the kitchen with a big cheesy grin.

'You look like the cat who got the cream,' Sarah laughs. 'Have you had a good day? Where did you go? Have you been to the tea house again? What's that over your trousers?' I reply to each question as best I can.

'Yes, I have got the cream; yes, I did have a good day; yes, I did go to the tea house and I spilt a cup of tea over myself.'

'That should have impressed Faye,' Sarah laughs.

'Well, I managed to get a date with her tomorrow night,' I say smugly.

'No wonder you look so pleased with yourself,' Rob joins in. 'You old dog.'

'That's great news!' Sarah exclaims.

'I'm going to phone her tonight to make arrangements,' I say. 'Do you know of a nice place to take her?'

'What sort of thing do you want to do?' Asks Rob. 'Dancing, out for a meal, or both?'

'Where did we used to go when we first met?' Sarah asks Rob.

'That was years ago.' Rob replies. 'Faye and Alex are too old for those sort of places.'

'There's a jazz night on at the "Three Stags" tomorrow and they serve good food,' suggests Sarah. 'I know Faye likes jazz.'

'Jazz sounds great to me. Oh and one more thing, can I borrow your car? Mine's in a bit of a state at the moment.'

'Faye's not the type of woman to care what sort of car you drive,' says Sarah. 'She drives an old Citroen.'

'I just want a little boost. It gives me a bit more confidence. I know it's shallow.'

'Let him take ours,' says Rob. 'We don't need it tomorrow night. We could have a romantic night in.'

'You can have the car,' says Sarah. 'But you should really have a bit more faith in yourself.'

'I've go more "Faith" than you could dream of.' I say, thinking back to my little problem.

'What?'

'Oh, nothing.'

'You used to be so full of confidence when you were younger. Sometimes a bit too much, from what I remember!'

'Yes I know. Just can't understand where it all went. Lost it over the years, I guess. That's what happens at our age, when you've been through the mill a few times.'

'You make yourself sound 80, Alex.'

'I feel 80 most of the time.'

'You do need this break, don't you,' says Rob.

'Do you two mind getting your own dinner tonight?' Asks Sarah, changing the subject. 'I'm having a girls' night in with Shauna and Faye. Shauna's thinking of changing her job.'

'No, we don't mind, do we Alex?' Rob replies for the both of us. 'I can cook a mean beans-on-toast.'

'With brown sauce and butter mixed in,' I add. 'Must have brown sauce.'

'No wonder you've put on weight. You can have whatever you like, as long as there are no pots and pans for me to wash up when I get home.' says Sarah

'Does anybody need to use the toilet before I get in the shower?' asks Rob.

'I do, I've been bursting to go for ages.'

'Looks like you've already been,' quips Sarah. 'Judging by the state of your trousers!' *If only she knew the truth.* I leave Rob and Sarah and go upstairs for a pee. On the way back down, Rob and I meet on the stairs.

'Do you think you could have a chat with Sarah?' Rob asks. 'You know, what we talked about last night.'

'Yes, sure, I'll talk to her now.'

'Thanks.'

Sarah is in the garden watering some hanging baskets.

'Sarah, can I have a word?' I approach sheepishly.

'Not more questions about Faye, please, just go out with her and see what happens.'

'No, it's not Faye, it's Rob.'

'What about Rob?' Sarah looks puzzled.

'Rob told me what the doctors said, about you not being able to have children.' Sarah's face drops. Her eyes fill with tears.

'Rob's worried, Sarah. He thinks you're trying to push him away. He did want children but he wants you a lot more. Rob loves you so much. He'd rather be with you than have children with anyone else.'

'When did he tell you all of this?' asks Sarah.

'Last night, when we were down the pub. Sarah, he doesn't blame you, he knows you'd love to have his baby. He's worried this is going to tear the two of you apart. He's struggling to find the strength, seeing you so sad all the time. Telling him that he should find someone else to have children with.'

'Rob's always loved the idea of having children,' Sarah's voice trembles. 'It's all we used to talk about when we first got married. I can't give him what he wants most in life.'

'You're what he wants most in life. Rob wouldn't swap you for the world.'

'If I'm what he wants, why does he spend all his time at

work? He seems not to want to spend as much time with me as he used to.'

'Rob's finding your sadness hard to cope with. He's scared that he's losing you. He thinks the less time you are together, the less chance there is for arguments to start. I know it's not the right way to sort out the problem but if you could have a bit more faith in him, in the love you share, it might take the pressure off him.'

'Take the pressure off him?' Tears flood down Sarah's face. 'Who's going to take the pressure off me?' I hold her and hug her close. We stand like this for a while, Sarah sobbing in my arms. As we enter the house, we hear Rob coming down the stairs. Sarah pulls away and hastily mops the tears from her eyes. She doesn't want Rob to see that she's been crying.

'Is everything Ok?' he asks, as he enters the room. Sarah rushes past him and runs upstairs.

'What did you say to her? I wanted you to reassure her, not upset her!' he says, eyebrows furrowed.

'I only spoke to her about what we talked about last night. She's very sad. Rob, you're both strong enough to get through this. Both of you need to stop hiding from the problem. You're always working, Sarah's always in the garden or round a friend's house. I think it's time to face the music.' Rob just looks at me in disbelief and walks out the room. *Who am I to be giving relationship advice? I've never made one last yet.* I can hear raised voices from upstairs! I think I've caused an argument. About an hour later, Sarah and Rob reappear. Sarah's dressed to go out. Rob walks through the lounge into his study. Sarah puts on a brave face and tries to smile.

'What time are you going out?' I ask.

'About 8:30. Shauna is coming round to pick me up.'

'Is everything alright between you two? I haven't upset the two of you have I? I was only trying to help.'

'We're alright.' I'm not convinced. Sarah's voice seems rather sombre. I say no more about the matter.

'Would you like a cup of tea, sis'?'

'Yes, that'd be lovely.'

'Shall I make one for Rob as well?'

'No, not just yet, he's got some work to look at. He hates being disturbed.' Sarah and I drink our tea in silence.

It's 8 o'clock, I am dying to phone Faye. *Wait a while,* I tell myself. Don't want to seem too desperate. I sit twiddling my thumbs, nervously.

'What's up?' asks Sarah. 'You seem on edge.'

'Nothing. I said I'd phone Faye at eight. Just giving it a little time, so I don't look desperate.'

'Don't be stupid,' Sarah tells me. 'Just phone her now and stop acting like some overgrown baby. Women don't think it's cool for men to pretend that they don't want to see us as much as we want to see them.' I take Faye's card out of my pocket, dial the number. I'm shaky. Hands sweating. I'm close to putting the phone down. Faye picks up before I do.

'Hello,' it's Faye's sweet voice on the other end.

'Hello, Faye, it's Alex. How are you? Have you had a good day?'

'Yes, thanks, some handsome chap came into the shop today and swept me off my feet.' I swell with pride, at this remark.

'I was phoning to arrange something for tomorrow night,' I say. 'I thought we could go out for a meal and the jazz night at the "Three Stags", if that's Ok with you.'

'That'd be great,' Faye says, excitedly. 'I love live jazz. I'll try not to pick at the cakes at work tomorrow, don't want to spoil my appetite.'

'Shall I pick you up about 8:30?' I ask.

'Could you make it 9? It takes me a while to finish up at work after closing. That would give me a little extra time to make myself look presentable.'

'I can't imagine you looking anything other than presentable.'

'Believe me, you haven't seen me with a few pints inside,' Faye chuckles. 'I'm anything but presentable.'

'Umm, sounds promising, I'll just have to make sure you have a few pints.'

'Why kind sir, I thought you were a gentleman. I must go now, your sister's coming round tonight. I'll get full background information on you then. See you tomorrow! Bye.'

'Bye Faith.'

'What? What did you call me?'

'Faye, I called you Faye. Bye then.' I put the phone down and smile at Sarah. She is ready to leave for her night out with the girls.

'Don't tell too many of my secrets.' I say to her.

'What makes you think that we're going to talk about you? We've got interests of our own you know. You'll have plenty of time to impress Faye yourself, tomorrow.'

'Just say one nice thing about me, just to get the ball rolling, tell her how interesting I am.'

'You're interesting alright,' she giggles. 'But purely as a psychiatric case.' My face drops, Sarah can see this remark has hurt me.

'I was only joking Alex. Don't be so sensitive. You used to be able to take a joke.'

'I'm sorry, sis, you're right.' Anyway, I think that my present mental state gives another side to my already complex character.'

'You'll be Ok.' Sarah reassures me. 'This little break should do you good. Who knows, you and Faye might hit it off.'

'If we do, she'll probably turn out to be a bit crazy. I seem to attract the odd ones. Charlie said that women would be the bane of my life, she's right so far.'

'Alex, you must move on from Charlie!' Sarah raises her voice. 'Why do you think that you're in such a state. You were never like this until you met that bitch. Can't you see that not all women are like Charlie? Some are sensitive and have feelings.'

'I don't want to get into an argument now. Charlie wasn't that bad, just a bit highly strung.'

'Highly strung, she was a fucking maniac!'

'I can't help who I fall in love with. Emotions don't always guide you in the best directions.'

'It wasn't your emotions guiding you with her, it was your cock.' I'm shocked to hear Sarah talk this way. 'Alex, I must go, Shauna has just pulled up,' says Sarah. 'Bye Rob,' she calls through to the study. I hear no reply.

'Do you think Rob is Ok?' I ask Sarah.

'He's fine, just leave him alone 'til he's ready to come out.' As soon as Sarah leaves, I feel a bit awkward. I hope I've not caused any problems. After all, Rob did ask me to have a word with her. It's not an easy thing to do, especially when they're both so upset about the subject.

I walk into the lounge and switch on the telly, flop down

on the sofa and breathe a big sigh. I should really go and shower and change but don't have the energy. Maybe a quick drink, then a shower. *Wow, what a day, talk about an emotional roller-coaster*, I think to myself. *I'm shattered.* It doesn't take long before I feel myself drifting off. This always happens when I put the telly on.

Seven.

All That Jazz.

This is it. This is my big night. My first date with Faye. Butterflies in my stomach, bees in my head. I'm so nervous, I'm so excited!

'For God's sake, sit down! You're making me nervous,' says Rob.

'I can't sit, my legs won't let me. I can't believe I'm going out with Faye tonight.'

'Alex, she's just a woman. You've been out with women before,' Rob is laughing. 'You've changed so much. When Sarah and I got married, you were flirting with all the woman guests at the wedding reception.'

'I was a lot younger then and I had all my hair.'

'You must have had a few shallow women in the last years. You never used to think like this. Faye obviously finds you attractive, she asked you out!'

'How do I look?'

'You look great! If I wasn't married to your sister I'd be after you myself.'

'Are you and Sarah busy tonight? Did you two want to come along?' Rob stares at me in disbelief.

'You're a big boy now, you don't need a chaperone,' Rob is laughing again.

'Sarah and I are having a night in, so don't rush home.'

'If I'm not home by two, I've struck it lucky or more likely taken the wrong turning and got lost.'

'Well, let's just hope it's the first option. If you do go back to Faye's, remember don't eat the cakes. You're confused enough already without the help of chemical additives.' We both laugh, Rob has a way of relaxing me.

'What are you two up to?' asks Sarah, as she enters the room. 'You look like a pair of naughty school boys who've just got caught smoking behind the bike sheds.'

'We were just talking about Faye. I think Alex feels lucky.'

'Alex, don't you rush things. Faye's not an old slapper, she's a good friend of mine and I don't want you upsetting her.'

'I would not insult her by pushing things too fast.'

'She's a good woman. Don't spoil things by going into some silly routine to hide your insecurities, just be yourself and you'll be Ok.'

'I think we should all lighten up a bit,' says Rob. 'This is supposed to be a night out for Alex and a romantic night in for us.' Sarah throws Rob a coy little glance.

8:30, comes around, I'm ready to go.

'I must be off. I have to pick Faye up at nine.'

'Have a great time,' says Rob. 'Drive carefully, the roads are narrow round here, don't want you scratching the car.'

'Remember, just be yourself and you'll have a good night,' says Sarah. I kiss her on the cheek.

'Thanks, sis'. I'll try my best to act normal. See you later Rob. You two have a nice night.' I walk out into the night and get into Sarah's car. Looking at the map, I try to find Polgooth. I'm crap at reading maps. I spot it on the map but it's still not clear to me. I turn on the ignition and head in the direction that I think I should be going. Gosh, the car is really nice to drive, so smooth, so clean. I'm into one track roads very shortly. It's a bit creepy, no street lights. I turn the stereo up for company. I have always wondered what would happen if I met a big tractor or lorry coming from the other direction. I wouldn't be able to reverse all the way back. The hedge rows leave no room to pull over. Moths the size of sparrows keep flying into the head lights. I keep the windows wound up so they don't join me in the car. Then caught in my head lights is Faith. She's flying ahead of the car. I put my foot down, trying to catch up with her. God, she can fly fast. Can't catch up with her. When suddenly she stops, turns to me and points. Looking in the direction that Faith is pointing. I see that I'm at Faye's place. It's a small cottage, just the sort of place I pictured her having. Looking round there is no sign of Faith.

'Stay away, just for tonight,' I plead.

It's only a quarter to nine. *Should I wait in the car or turn up early? Remember what Sarah said,* "Just be yourself". I walk to the front door and look for the bell. There isn't one. So I lift the door knocker. It's made from solid brass. It's in the form of a goblin. The knocker's stiff. I struggle to bang it down. The first attempt I manage to catch my fingers between the knocker and the door.

'Ah fa fa!' I yelp. Changing hands I try again, this time it strikes the door, with the sound of thunder. I wait for ages. Eventually, Faye opens the door. She has a towel wrapped around her slender body.

'Did you knock?' she asks sarcastically. 'You're a little early, I have not added the finishing touches yet.'

'Sorry about that, I didn't want to sit in the car in the dark. It didn't take me as long to find your house as I thought it would.'

'Come in, I won't be much longer. Have a seat in the lounge,' Faye gestures for me to sit down. As she leaves the room, the towel catches on the door handle to reveal the peachiest little bottom. I turn to jelly and start getting in a fluster. I'm doing somersaults in my boxer shorts. *Calm down Alex.... You've seen an bum before .... Yes, I know but not one quite like Faye's .... I said calm down.* I realise I'm arguing with myself, I think I'm losing it. After about ten minutes Faye re-appears in the lounge, looking stunning. She's wearing a light blue, pearlescent, mid-length dress, with straps at the shoulders. Her eyes look even bluer in this dress. I wouldn't have thought it possible, this is the sort of woman you dream about.

'Wow! You look fantastic!'

'Thank you,' Faye smiles. 'You don't look so bad yourself. Just one thing, can I check your socks?' I start to lift my trouser legs.

'I don't really want to see them,' Faye, giggles.

'You'll have to show me the way tonight, I don't know the area,' I say.

'I have every intention of showing you the way!' says Faye, with a glint in her eye. I feel myself getting excited. My cock's getting lobby. *Lazarus has arisen.*

'We'd better get going.' I say with urgency.

'Ok, just let me get my hand-bag.' We walk in silence to the car. Every now and then Faye brushes her arm against mine. *Is it my imagination or do I keep getting static shocks from her?*

'Your carriage awaits, mademoiselle.' I open the car door and take Faye's hand as she sits, then I close the door behind her. I walk round the car trying to be as cool as possible. Inside I'm a mass of neuroses, my legs turn to jelly. As I sit in the car, I turn to Faye. To my surprise, she's lighting up two cigarettes.

'I assume you smoke, too,' she says.

'Yes, thank goodness you do too, at least I don't have to keep running off to the toilets for a sly fag tonight.'

'It makes the first kiss a lot easier too,' grins Faye, grabbing me and kissing me full on the lips. 'Now, we don't have to worry when to make a move, it's already out in the open.'

'Let's get going, if we hang round here much longer, I might just whisk you back to the house.'

'Be patient, we have all the time in the world.' Faye looks deep into my eyes. *What can she see?* I wonder. Her eyes strip my soul bare. I start the car. Taking the cigarette from Faye, I inhale the smoke deep into my lungs and hold it for a while. Right at this moment life feels good. We drive through the country lanes with full beams ablaze. There's magic in the air, or is it just me getting swept away by the moment? "Nat King Cole" playing on the stereo.

The atmosphere is definitely electric. Faye has a look of excitement on her face. As I park the car, I hear music from the pub. The entertainment's already started. I recognise the tune, it's "Strut Miss Lizzie". Sounds like it could be a good night. We enter the pub, there are people dancing and clapping. This is my kind of place.

'What would you like to drink?' I ask Faye.

'I'll have a pint of 'Six X', please,' she replies. My face must have shown my shock.

'You're not in the city now Alex. Us country girls like a pint sometimes.'

'Nice pint, isn't it? Rob and I had a few last night.'

'I'll grab the seats over there while you get the drinks in. We're lucky there're some left this time of night.' I walk to the bar, the place is packed. They have a fantastic choice of real ale. In my younger days, I would have tried them all. A ruddy-faced bar man serves me. I wonder to myself, *Is it drink or is he a musician? Maybe he plays the trumpet, a trumpet that has given him that complexion.* I stick to the 'Six X'. Some of these real ales are pretty strong. I don't want to make a fool of myself. I get the drinks and take them over to the table that Faye's secured for us. As soon as I put the drinks down, she grabs hers and downs about half of it in one, long, unfeminine gulp.

'Were you thirsty?' I ask, taking a sip of my beer.

'Yes, you would be too, if you'd spent the day in a hot tea shop.' I take the seat next to her. She slides closer. 'I haven't been to a live show for ages, it's so much better then a juke box.' She says.

'Is there live music here all the time?'

'They have live bands probably about once a month. It's very quiet the other nights, a completely different atmosphere to the place.'

'I could get used to this, good music, good beer, a pretty woman. A man doesn't need much else in life.'

'How old did you say you were? 70, was it?'

'Yeah, suppose I asked for that. I did sound like a comfortable old slipper.'

'Well, don't get too comfortable. Did you know you can dance to jazz music?'

'Did you know, I can't dance to anything? I've got two left feet!'

'Don't be daft, anybody can dance. Just listen to the rhythm, follow me. I won't let you go wrong,' Faye drags me onto the dance floor. Before long, we're dancing. I've never been able to dance, yet here I am, dancing like I've been dancing for years.

'I told you, you could dance, you just needed the right partner. Play your cards right, I'll teach you some more moves tonight.' I could feel myself blush. I think I might be out of my depth with this intoxicating nymph. The song comes to an end, we return hand in hand to our seats. The band front man introduces the next song.

'Thank you,' says the man with the clarinet. 'The next song is a favourite of mine, hope you enjoy it as much as I do. Ladies and gentlemen, "Lilacs In The Rain". A loud cheer goes up, with clapping from the whole pub. A lot more couples get up to dance. Faye and I miss out this one and try to have a conversation. The music is loud, so I don't catch everything she says. A lot of the time I'm just nodding and smiling, hoping these gestures are all in the right place!

'The restaurant is just through that door. We'd better go through soon, last food orders are 10:00,' Faye tells me. We get up and walk into the dinning area. I'm surprised how big it is. The music is at a better level in here: the speakers are set at a lower volume. The menus are on the table.

'What do you recommend?' I ask.

'Well, I'm a veggie, so I'll be having the vegetable cannelloni.'

'Sounds good to me, what about a starter?'

'No, no, have to watch my weight.'

'There's nothing of you. You should try to carry a belly like mine around.'

'There'd be a lot more of me, if I had a starter and a sweet. I pile it on if I eat too much. Anyway, I want to dance some more after we've eaten.'

'Tell me about yourself, I know nothing about you. How long have you known Sarah?'

'I met Sarah and Rob shortly after they moved down here. They came into the tea house. Sarah and I struck up an instant friendship.'

'How long have you lived here?'

'I've lived here for as long as I can remember, seems like forever.'

'Have you never thought about living anywhere else?'

'Yes, I've thought about it but never got round to doing anything about it. I'm a simple person. I'm happy with my tea shop. As long as I can go home at the end of the day, listen to music, relax with the girls occasionally.'

'What about men, is there a man in your life? Have I got to fight a duel to win your heart?'

'No, no man, the path is clear.'

'Have you never been married or lived with anybody? You're a very beautiful woman, you must have had someone special.' Faye falls silent for a short while.

'There has been someone special for a long time but he was totally unaware that I was on this earth. I've just been waiting for him to fall for me.'

'I thought you said the path was clear.'

'You're the man I've been waiting for, the one I've wanted for the last twenty odd years.'

'Me? How can it be me? You've only just met me. We haven't known each other for twenty years.'

'I said that you didn't know I was on this earth. I've been hanging around all this time for you, to come to me.' *Uh-oh, crazy woman alert,* once more I have managed to fall for a complete loony.

'What do you mean, waiting for me?'

'I've never met a man who I fancied, like I fancy you. I've tried but I've never clicked with anybody else. I just feel we'd be right together, something in me says it's right with you.' I don't say this to Faye, but for some reason I've had the same feeling. Past experience tells me to pull back from this woman. My foolish heart (or is it my loins), wants me to stay.

'Well, let's just see where the night takes us.'

The order takes about twenty minutes to arrive. It's well worth the wait. I also order a bottle of Chardonnay. I can only drink a glass of this as I'm driving, so Faye drinks the rest. The wine doesn't seem to affect her at all. If I were to drink that much, I'd be on the floor.

'It's Ok, my ancestors were Italian!' Faye exclaims.

'I think my ancestors must have been Puritans. Three pints and I'm anybody's.'

'Only two more to get you,' says Faye. 'Then you're mine for the night.'

'Sorry, I can't drink any more, I'm driving, you'll just have to have me sober.' As soon as we finish our meal, Faye wants to go back into the bar for a dance. I surprise myself, I'd usually protest. Dancing all night long is not usually the way I behave. Somehow it feels right with Faye. Apart from the static shocks I keep getting from her.

'Is this going to happen every time I touch you? It's lucky I don't have a pacemaker.'

'Stop moaning. It's good when the sparks fly.' As we spin around the floor, I am enveloped in electricity. I find myself staring into Faye's eyes. I am uncontrollably drawn to this woman. *I want her. God, how I want her!*

'I want you too,' Faye tells me.

'What?'

'I said, I want you too.'

'How did you know what I was thinking?'

'You weren't thinking, Alex. You said, you want me.'

'I didn't hear me say it. But I'll take your word on it.'

I'm not sure what time the entertainment went on to but it was certainly gone midnight when we left to go home. I drive back to Faye's slowly. I just don't want the night to end. I'm feeling a little reluctant to drop her off yet. This is the first time in ages that I've felt this way about anybody.

'Fancy a night cap?' Faye asks. 'Just promise to be good.'

'That'd be nice. I can't have any more alcohol, it'll have to be a coffee.' As we step through the door, Faye slips off her shoes. I follow her into the kitchen. She fills the kettle, plugs it in. Then she turns, wrapping her arms around my shoulders, kisses me deep in the mouth. Again, I can feel the static shocks shooting between us.

'You could stay the night, my bed's big enough for two' Faye's eyes pull me in. I can't resist, I don't want to resist. She leads me by the hand up the stairs to the bedroom. She turns to me, kisses me on the lips once more. 'Unzip me,' she commands, softly. I am shaking with anticipation. The zipper of her dress glides down smoothly, the dress falls to the floor. To my delight, Faye is wearing no under garments. I pull her towards me, as I do, I get more static shocks.

'Why does that always happen when I touch you? Have you got bad electrics here as well?'

'Shut up Alex, Just take me, no more talking.' We crash onto the bed. I can only describe the love making that follows as something out of this world. As we take pleasure from each other the static shocks became more intense, nearly painful, a pleasurable pain, a pain that I do not want to stop. Strange images keep flitting in to my head. It seems I am watching our love making as well as participating in it. I can see our bodies writhing in pain and pleasure, bathed in a bright blue light. We were not in Faye's bedroom anymore. We are on another plane. Wrapped in intense blue light. The only sensation is our bodies, taking pleasure from each other. Grinding for all I'm worth. Reaching our highest point in unison. We give out loud animalistic screams of ecstasy. Then we fall to the bed exhausted, sweating. If there ever was a time to die, it was now. Nothing else I would do in the future could come close to the sex of tonight. I lie on my back for quite some time, just staring at the ceiling. I'm sure I have a silly grin on my face. I turned to face Faye, she's asleep with her back to me. I caress her back, I notice two large raised scars between her shoulder blades, they are uniform, perfect symmetry. I wonder what had caused them. I touch the scares with my finger tips. As I do Faye winces and groans. I pull my hands away quickly, I don't want to wake her. *How did she get the scares?...They don't look like scares caused by an accidental injury....Maybe they are body art, cut intentionally.* Very soon I could feel myself sinking into sleep with Faye wrapped in my arms.

Eight.

Ulterior Motive.

'Wake up sleepy head!' I say, shaking Faye by the shoulder. 'You're going to be late for work if you don't get up soon.'

'Arghh, no, leave me to sleep. I'm shattered,' Faye mumbles. 'Shauna's going to open up for me today. Just go back to sleep.'

'I should be getting back to Sarah, she'll be wondering where I am!'

'No she won't, she'll guess you stayed over.' Faye is still mumbling. 'Snuggle in and go back to sleep.' This idea sounds good to me. I slide back to Faye's side of the bed. Immediately I feel my cock twitching.

'You can give that thought up. I'm still whacked from last night,' Faye protests.

'Sorry, can't help it, that thing has a mind of its own.'

'Well, tell it to get its mind on something else, either going back to sleep or making a pot of tea.' I opt for going back to the land of dreams. What strange dreams they are. One moment I'm running through a forest, being chased by shadowy strangers. The next I'm soaring through the air on the back of a giant bird, chasing Faith as she flies away from me. Over mountains, gliding along cold fresh valleys. Swooping down to crystal clear rivers, back up into the clouds. I could touch the hand of God if I reached out. Everything is so clear, so clean, the air so fresh. Then suddenly, for no reason the majestic bird turns into a chicken. The chicken with me clinging tightly around its neck, plummets towards the ground at tremendous speed.

'No!' I wake with a scream, nearly knocking Faye out of bed.

'For God's sake, are you mad?'

'I'm so sorry, I was having a dream that turned into a nightmare.' I explain the dream.

'Flying dreams are supposed to be a sign of a healthy mind,' she says. 'I don't know what falling with a big chicken dreams mean. Maybe they mean that you're just plain bonkers.' Faye gets out of bed. I can't help but stare at her bum. I want to bite it.

'Turn around, I want a good look.' Faye turns. Her tits are perfect, tight little belly. My eyes glide down towards her fuzzy triangle.

'Come here.'

'No you have to wait, you horny toad.' Faye leaves the room to go down stairs. I don't know what she's done but I'm solid. I thought erections were a thing of the past.

'Would you like a cup of tea, my magnificent stallion?' Faye shouts from the kitchen. I hear her laughing.

'Yes please, I just have to trot to the toilet first.' While I'm in the bathroom, I give myself an appraisal in the mirror. *You don't look too bad, for a man of your age.* Turning sideways, looking at my reflection, I pull my stomach in. *Some women like a bit of cuddle muscle!* I try to repeat some of the dance moves from last night and bang my knee on the shower door.

'Ow, ow.'

'Are you Ok, up there?'

'Yes. I'll be down in a minute. When I join Faye downstairs, she's sitting at the dinning table, reading a paper. She's wearing a skimpy top that reveals the scars on her back. I'd forgotten all about them. *Should I ask about them?... That might embarrass her.* I've not known her long enough to pry into her business. *Surely if she was ashamed of the scars, she'd hide them....She might have just forgotten to cover them up....Look, this is a woman who's not worried about what others think....* Curiosity gets the better of me.

'The scars on your back, how did they happen?'

'To tell the truth Alex, I've brought you back here to reveal more to you than just the scars. You're going to have the ride of your life today. You can take that look off your face, this ride has nothing to do with sex!'

'I was not thinking about sex.' (I'm lying of course.) 'I'm intrigued, pray tell me more.'

'Let's have some tea and toast,' says Faye. 'Hopefully, you'll be able to spend the rest of the day with me. That'll give us plenty of time to go on a voyage of discovery.' Then I remembered what Rob told me, about Faye being into tarot cards and other such mystic nonsense.

'Are you going to read my palm? If so remind me to wash my hands first, I don't want you digging up the dirt!'

'No, not palm reading, what I have to tell you is far more unbelievable than that.'

We finish breakfast in a relaxed silence, this is something that I couldn't do with many people. It just feels right with Faye. I know this sounds corny but I feel that I've known her all my life. She stands and walks out of the room.

'I'm going to have a shower. You can join me, if you reach the bathroom before I lock the door.' I'm up, out of my seat like a jack-in-a-box, taking two stairs at a time. I reach the bathroom a split second after Faye.

'My, you're keen!' Off comes what little clothing we're wearing. The shower is turned on full power (and so am I). Faye grabs me and pulls me into the shower.

'Now, take me like you did last night, don't spare the horses.' This woman is not of this world, as soon as we embrace the sparks start flying, the water cascading over our bodies only serves to intensify the electricity. My body is writhing with extreme pain and extreme pleasure. Every fibre of my being is burning, tingling. At the height of our passion, Faye takes my head in her hands and looks deep within me. Pictures from my past flash before my eyes: Mum, Dad, Sarah as a child, me as a child, chickens, my teens, my first girlfriend, my first job, my first sexual experience, my babies being born, fairies, angels. These images are mixed with images of what seems to be someone else's life, images of fairies and goblins, things I don't understand. *How did Faye get all that information about me? How does she know what my life has been. Does she read minds? I always felt that something was unusual about me. Maybe I'm not as mad as I thought. The fairy I saw as a child, the fairy at the window the other night. Seeing Faith these last few days. The strange feelings that I've had since arriving at Sarah's. Do all these things really exist? How can Faye show me these things, just by looking deep into my eyes. Surely all this is a dream. I must be unconscious in some hospital, I must wake up!*

'What the hell's going on?' I've pulled myself from her grasp, I am sprawled on the bathroom floor. 'What did you just do to me?'

'I'm sorry Alex, I was just reminding you of things from the past, things that you have forgotten.'

'Forgotten, how can I forget? I've spent a lifetime, thinking that I'm mad. I'm on medication due to all this. I haven't told my doctor half the story. I've spent the last thirty odd years trying to hide from these memories.'

'I am so very sorry! It was insensitive of me to show you in this fashion. I just couldn't control myself. I wanted you to share everything with me, not just the physical but the spiritual. That was my life you saw as well.'

'You could've warned me!' I protest. 'I'm not mentally at my strongest at the moment.'

'Please forgive me, I didn't want to frighten you.' She looks sad, pathetic, it's impossible to stay angry with her. I'm beginning to calm down. I've just seen my life in wide screen and it was a bit of a jolt.

'Please don't be angry with me, it's just that you have to be primed for what I have to tell you next. Prepare yourself for a big shock Alex.'

'Primed, what do you mean "primed"? I'm not a bomb!'

'You were brought here for a reason. There's someone who wants to meet you.' Faye is serious now. 'Alex, you have a daughter, whom you've never met.'

'You crazy bitch! What are you on about?' I shout.

'I don't have another daughter, it's impossible. I would know if I'd gotten someone pregnant. None of my ex's were pregnant and last night was the first one night stand I've had in a long time.'

'Thank you very much! Is that all it was to you. A one night stand? You don't know how long I've been waiting for you.'

'Faye stop it, we've only just met, how can you have been waiting for me?'

'You have only just met me but I've been watching you for a long time.' I'm getting worried, I look round to make sure there are no sharp objects near. I must have a crazy magnet, I always attract the nutters.

'Please, Alex, just give me a chance to explain. I know it all sounds very strange but you know there are other things to this world, things out of the ordinary.'

'Yes, unfortunately, they all turn out to be my girlfriends! I can't go through another mad relationship. I've not properly recovered from the last.'

'I'm not mad. What you are about to hear is going to take some faith on your part. You believe in fairies, don't you.'

'Oh, very funny, I suppose you and Sarah have been having a great laugh at my expense.'

'Sarah knows nothing of this. She must never know!' Faye exclaims. 'This all started long ago. I'll show you proof. You won't need too much convincing, because you already know a lot more than most.'

'Please, Faye don't do this to me,' I can feel all the worries from the past flooding back to haunt me. 'I'm not strong enough to take any more weird things in my life.'

'When you have the full story, you'll be Ok,' Faye reassures me. I get the urge to bolt for the door, something is keeping me from doing so. Maybe it's my state of mind. I need to know that all the strange things that have happened to me, did happen to me.

'Look, just take ten minutes to compose yourself,' Faye is trying to calm me down. 'I have a lot of stuff to show you which should allay your doubts.'

'How can I have a daughter that I don't know about? I have always taken my children and responsibilities very seriously. I can't believe that I'm even considering listening to you.'

'You weren't to know. I have to show you, for any of this to make any sense. Come with me. If anything is too distressing let me know and I'll try my best to make it easier.'

We dry ourselves and return to the bedroom. I have to put on the same clothes that I wore last night. Faye slips on a black skirt and pale blue blouse. I follow her through to the back of the house. At one end of the dinning room is a door.

'This leads to the cellar,' explains Faye. 'Don't worry, I promise that I am not a mad axe murderer. I have to keep everything down here out the way of prying eyes.

'You're not one of those dominatrix mistresses with a dungeon, are you?'

'Well, I might be but this has nothing to do with that side of my life.' She's trying to lighten the moment. I must admit, at this moment in time, I'm not at all sure about Faye's sanity. I think she may well be just as mad as me. The question is, do I follow her down into the basement or do I make a run for it whilst I still can?

Nine.

Deeper and Deeper.

Being the fool I am, I decide to follow Faye down the stairs. My curiosity always gets the better of me. Faye leads me by the hand. As she takes hold of me, I get the usual shock from her.

'Has this static thing got anything to do with your secret?'

'Yes, it has everything to do with it and the scars,' Faye smiles. 'Everything will become clear in good time. Don't look so scared.'

'I have every reason to be scared. So many disturbing things have happened to me over this past week.' My voice has a slight tremble that I try to hide. To my surprise, the basement is very bright. I was expecting a dark, damp, musty room: this is the complete opposite. The air in the room has a turquoise mist that floats around. The walls are painted white and the floor is a light wood.

There are a lot of books on shelves, not much furniture, just a small leather-look sofa and a coffee table. The atmosphere is very calming.

'Sit down, relax.' Faye points to the sofa. I get the strangest feeling that I am under her hypnotic control. 'You will feel a little strange at first but that sensation will soon go.'

'Have you hypnotised me, Faye? I seem to know what I am doing but I'm not sure that I am doing it of my own free will.'

'No, you're fully conscious, it's just the magic in the room that sharpens the senses. You will become aware of your mind and body, more than you ever have been in your life.' I can't help thinking that I should be disturbed by the things she is saying. For some reason, it all seems perfectly acceptable. Faye picks a large book from one of the shelves, which she opens in front of me.

'Where did you get that from?' In the book is a photograph of my daughter Jay, when she was about sixteen. 'Have you been following her as well?'

'Look closer.' I studied the photo for a long time. It is Jay but there seems to be something different, something I can't quite put my finger on.

'Alex, this is Donna, she is your daughter, the one I was telling you about.'

'I know for a fact that I don't have a daughter called Donna. Please explain to me, how you think I had a child without my knowledge. That picture is of Jay. I want to know how you come to have it.'

'Look at the eyes, you can see it's not Jay. Donna was conceived around the same time as Jay but they have different mothers.'

'Are you trying to tell me that I had sex with someone, without knowing? I know I'm forgetful but even I would notice a woman wrapped round my penis.'

'This is the hard part. Some of your sperm was taken from you when you were younger. It was used to fertilise the egg that Donna came from.'

'How do you mean taken from me? I don't leave my sperm lying around for all and sundry to scoop up, to use willy nilly.'

'I am going to try and explain as best I can,' says Faye, laughing. 'Your sperm was taken from you while you slept. It has been happening for years, not just to you. It happened, is happening to a lot of men. Have you ever wondered why men awake so often with an erection? You are going to laugh at this next part. Female fairies' are slipping under your sheets at night, masturbating the males of your species. They collect the end result to fertilise fairy eggs.'

'Can you tell me just one thing Faye, how long have you been using hallucinogenic substances?' I can't believe Faye actually thinks that I'm that stupid. 'For what reason do fairies' need my juice, are all the male fairies' gay?'

'No they're not gay but they have become infertile over the last century.' She's back in serious mode now. 'We think it has been caused by all the pollutants in the environment. "Our species" was in danger of dying out.'

'What do you mean "Our species"? Are you trying to tell me that you are a fairy?'

'Yes, Alex. I am one of the first successful, fairy-human hybrids. Humans weren't our first choice. Because of the size difference, we have to incubate outside the fairy womb. This practice took many years to perfect.'

'So, what you are saying, is that you're a test tube baby. I don't believe that I'm having this conversation.'

'Kind of a test tube baby, only we fairies' use chickens eggs. Because the eggs are organic we can make them grow to accommodate the foetus as it develops.'

'Faye, please stop, this is all too much for me, either you're mad or I'm mad or we're both mad.'

'I'm sorry. Am I going too fast for you? It's just that there is so much to tell you. I know it all sounds incredible.'

'Incredible, it sounds insane! How am I supposed to believe all this nonsense?'

'I told you that it would be the ride of your life.' Faye takes my hand. 'Just open your mind, you've already seen things in your life that very few humans get to see. What I disclose to you today could get me into serious trouble. There are forces out there that want none of this disclosed. I'm not sure how far they are prepared to go, to keep this all locked away.'

'Forces? I don't think that MI5 really care about the lives of a woman who runs a tea house and a mad man.' Being sarcastic is the only way I can cope with this situation. 'I don't think that we are a threat to the Government! Do you?'

'Please try and take me seriously. I am laying myself bare here, mostly for your benefit. I have feelings too.' A tear runs down Faye's cheek, I lean towards her, mop it with my finger, it's warm. I put the tear to my lips and sip. The warm saltiness of her tear, consumes me. Why do I love this woman? Sense should be telling me to run to the other side of the earth. But I have no sense. All I have is an overwhelming love for a woman I barely know.

'I have to have a cigarette. Do you mind?'

'You'll have to leave the cellar, you can't smoke down here.' I climb the stairs and make my way to the kitchen, I put the kettle on, I'm going to need a cup of coffee as well. I stand staring out of the window. *What have I let myself in for now? Is there not a normal, safe woman out there for me. Someone who just wants a quiet life, no adventures, no arguments, no affairs?* Then I remember that I've had women like that. I nearly died of boredom. I only seem attracted to women who drive me crazy. At least no two days are the same with this type of woman. You never feel old with these women; exhausted but never old. The coffee and cigarette start to work, I'm beginning to relax again. I suppose I should go back down the cellar, see what else Faye has in store for me.

Ten.

Even Deeper.

While I'm away, Faye's taken the opportunity to gather together more evidence to convince me. The table's covered with all sorts of papers, photos and a large grey stone.

'You've been busy, what's all this stuff?'

'This is proof, everything I need to convince you that neither of us are mad!' Faye retorts. 'Documentary, photographic, most of all physical. You do believe your own eyes, don't you?'

'I've not believed my eyes since I was five years old. They keep showing me things that no one else can see. They are the biggest liars I've met to date.' Faye lifts the large stone from the table.

'This, my sweet sceptic, is a fossil. Only a few fossils are known to exist. It's the fossil of a fairy, one and half million years old. We have been around a long time.' She hands me the stone. On it is what looks like a tiny human figure. Only, it has wings. It could be a dragon fly.

'That's a clay sculpture, anyone could have made this in a pottery class.'

'It's not clay, Alex. Feel the weight, the texture. It's rock.' It is heavy and rough.' I inspect the rock thoroughly. The rock is brown and grey, it is sharp in places. The frozen figure would be difficult to make. I don't want to admit it but it does look real. Faye takes it back.

'Fairy fossils are very rare because a pure fairy is only visible when it wants to be. This one must have been caught out 'mid-glamour.'

'What's 'mid-glamour'?'

'This is the term that fairies' use for showing themselves to others. That's the static shocks you get from me. As I'm a hybrid I can't turn off my 'glamour'.'

'So that's never going to stop then. Whenever I'm with you, I'm going to be in pain. Is that what you're saying?'

'It's an electrical charge that makes fairies' visible. Very few people can see fairies' without this electrical charge being released. You're one of these people. When you hit your head all those years ago, it opened up a tiny fraction of your brain that humans keep tightly shut. Some people have this opening when they are born, others develop it. Like you, some have it thrust upon them.'

'If the fossil is not fake and you are a fairy, why is it so much smaller than you?'

'She was a pure breed. As I've told you, I'm of mixed race. Because my father was human, I've taken on some of the physical attributes of my human ancestry.' Faye seems to believe all she's telling me. I am not, for obvious reasons totally convinced. But the electric shock's that make our love making so fantastic, are something I've never experienced with any of my other girlfriends.

'I can't believe I'm actually considering that what you're telling me, could have any credibility.'

'Why would I want to make it up? What about Faith? You saw her.'

'How do you know about Faith?'

'I sent her to you.'

'You sent her? But she's a real fairy, won't she tell the powers that be?

'She's safe. Faith is just a projection spell. She doesn't exist in reality.' I am disappointed at this statement.

'So I won't see her again, is that what you're saying?'

'No, you won't see her again. But you will see a lot more of me. Alex, I have waited a long time to show you all this.'

'If my mind's been opened, why aren't I seeing fairies' everywhere I go?'

'A clairvoyant doesn't see the dead all day long, only when he or she is concentrating. When was the last time you saw a badger? You know badgers exist. They don't have the power of being invisible, when the mood takes.'

'That's true.'

'It's the same with you. With the knowledge that I have given you, if you sat in your garden at night. Opened your mind, you would see many fairies'.' Faye, walks over to the sofa that I'm sat on and rests her hands on my knees.

'Just look all around your chicken house. You'll see them taking any eggs that haven't been collected.' Faye removes her blouse, turns her back to me.

'The scars on my back are not scars, look closely at them.

You'll see that the skin has never been broken, they are wing stumps. Some hybrids still grow wings, I am not sure if mine are going to develop fully or just stay like this.' I can't tell if they are scars or not, it's true that they are perfectly symmetrical which would be unusual for scars caused by an accident. I touch the marks. They tingle, it feels as if there's something under the skin. The only comparison I can make is they feel like a cyst. I become aware that Faye is groaning.

'Are you Ok? Did that hurt?' Faye heaves a big sigh.

'No, that doesn't hurt, quite the opposite, the stumps are very sensitive. I will have to ask you to stop, I'm getting turned on. We've not got time to make love. Shauna's coming round with Donna soon.' This statement hits me like a bolt of lightening. *What is Faye thinking?... How does she expect me to meet Donna today?... I've only just learned of her existence.*

'Donna, the girl you say is my daughter......,' I'm panicking 'I'm not ready to meet her yet. 'I've only just found out that she thinks she's mine.'

'She does not think, Alex, she knows,' Faye is furious. 'She's yours, there's no mistaking. Donna even has some of your mannerisms. Please give her a chance.'

'Give her a chance. What about giving me a chance? I only got here a couple of days ago. Now I have a new daughter?'

'I know you will love her as much as you love your other children. If I didn't think that were the case, I wouldn't have let Donna get in contact with you. It's a terrible risky business for all concerned.'

'Why is it risky? What could happen?'

'Your meeting Donna is a strict breach of Council rules.

We're not allowed to give any humans the knowledge that I've given you today. I'm not sure how far The Council are prepared to go to keep this secret. I've never heard of any other fairy child meeting his or her human parent before. The Council, over the years, have made it known that they would look upon any such incident as a serious crime against the Fairy Kingdom. They would consider it treason and we would be dealt with accordingly.'

'This is all a bit too far fetched for me, "Fairy Kingdoms", "treason"' I'm almost laughing. 'What are they going to do to us? Turn us into toads!'

'Stop it Alex! You know what I'm telling you is true, so why are you trying to deny it? I don't know what they'll do to Donna and me but I know they have the power to make you go mad. At least that'll be how it looks to everyone else. They could turn your mind inside out. You won't know what is the truth and what is fiction.'

'I'm already in that position. I've been like it for most of my life. Ever since the day I saw my first fairy. Can you imagine what it was like for a five year old? After the reaction I got from my parents. I dare not mention it to anybody else. I've kept all this pent up inside for such a long time. Is it any wonder that I'm seeing the doctor for happy pills every month?"

'This could be far worse than anything that you've experienced so far. I wouldn't risk it if I thought that it wasn't worth it. Donna wants to meet you. It's my fault. I've kept her informed all her life, on what you're like, what you were doing.'

'What have I been doing? I've been stuck in a job that I hate, for the last seventeen years. Wasting my life. Why would she want to be part of that?'

'She needs you, Alex. I need you. I'm willing to risk everything to be with you, I've waited too long. Despite what The Council says, I think we should be able to choose who we love.'

'How can I bring you and Donna into my life? What do I tell my children, the rest of my family? 'James, Jay, Peter, meet my new girlfriend, she's a fairy and oh, by the way, you have a sister who's a fairy too.' They would march me straight to the madhouse.'

'You're being silly now, we would break it to them gently, only your children would have to know, there's no reason to tell the rest of your family.'

'Break it to them gently, like you did to me? If that's you being gentle, I'd hate to see you on a clumsy, thoughtless day.'

'I didn't have enough time to be gentle with you. We think The Council might already be on to us. I want both of you to meet before someone puts a stop to it. Whatever happens, promise me that you'll take care of Donna.' We are interrupted by a loud banging at the door.

'That will be Shauna and Donna,' Faye tells me, as if it's the most natural thing in the world. 'Now stay calm. I will bring them to you. You won't regret this, I promise you.' Faye leaves me on my own, I'm shaking. I reach into my pocket for my cigarettes and lighter. In my nervousness, I drop most of the cigarettes on to the floor. Picking one up, I put it in my mouth. I try to light it but the lighter won't work. I'm really panicking now. I want to leave but my legs won't let me, they're stuck, they've turned to lead. I can hear voices on the stairway. The sweat running from my forehead stings my eyes. I can feel my heart racing, beating in my temples, in my chest, like a runaway steam train. I hear loud footsteps coming from the stairway. Faye reappears through the door. She has a young girl by her side.

'Alex, this is Donna.' Faye leads the girl into the room. 'Donna this is your father.' I stand up, immediately fall back on to the sofa, I can't believe my eyes. Donna looks just like Jay. I see only slight differences, Donna is an inch or two smaller than Jay. Her eyes are just a shade lighter. My God, she's my daughter, there's no doubt. Donna looks just as shocked as I am. I stand again, hold out my arms. Donna grabs me, we are stuck like this. Neither of us can talk. All we can do is hold each other and sob. I'm getting static shocks from Donna now.

'We'll leave you two alone for a while,' says Faye. She walks back towards the stairway with another woman. I didn't notice this other woman come into the room. There's a look of great happiness on Faye's face as she turns, before she leaves the room. Donna and I are still sobbing in each other's arms. I want to speak but can't find the words. After what seems an eternity, I manage to speak her name.

'Donna.'

'Daddy, how I've missed you!' Her voice is like angels' singing. 'Don't ever leave me again.'

'Oh, my sweet little girl, I'll never let you go.' I am sobbing uncontrollably. 'Never let you go.' I pull back, just enough to look her in the eyes. She's a replica of Jay. Same mouse brown hair. Pale blue eyes. She's even got the same tiny button nose that Jay has. Donna looks so much more delicate than Jay, if that's possible. Jay is a tiny, sweet, pretty thing. Donna looks like she'd shatter into a thousand shards if I held her too tight. I feel cheated that I've missed so much of her life. I've not had the chance to be there for her when she was unwell, when she cut her first teeth, when she took her first step. I've missed it all.

'Daddy, I can show you all that. You won't miss a thing.'

'How did you know what I was thinking?'

'I can hear your thoughts,' Donna starts to cry again. 'I've been able to hear your thoughts for most of my life. I could never see you, never be with you, never hold you, until now. You're just how I pictured you.'

'I never knew about you until today, I promise. Had I known you existed, I would have come for you.' I'm still sobbing. 'You have a sister and two brothers. You're just like your sister, Jay.'

'I know. I can feel them as well. How I've longed to meet them!' We're both beginning to calm down after the initial shock. 'I've wished to be with my family for as long as I can remember.'

'Well, this is one wish I can grant you, you'll never be apart from us again. Two girls, that's going to even the score a bit at home.'

'Home!' Donna beams. 'I'm going home!' What I'm feeling is so hard to explain. It's as if all the love that's been missed out on all these years has just filled the room. Twenty two years of love in a flickering of an eye. I have another daughter, someone who needs my protection, my love, my life. Now I need her as much as she needs me. I need to find out all about her. What her life has been. Is this vision before me, the thing in my life that I couldn't quite put my finger on. The feeling that something was missing? Is Donna the missing part of the jigsaw?

'God, you are beautiful, I'm so sorry I've missed you

growing up. Had I known about you, nothing in this world could have kept me from you. I will make it up to you, I promise.'

'Daddy, don't apologise, it's not your fault, you weren't to know,' she hugs me again. 'I've wanted to see you all these years, it wasn't possible.'

'Why? What do you mean 'not possible'? Just because I was in relationships, that doesn't mean you couldn't have come to me. You didn't have to wait 'til I was single before you came to me, you're my daughter. Nothing is more important than that.'

'Oh Daddy, I love you,' Donna sobs. 'I have my daddy now, that's all that matters to me. All I've been able to do over the years is to tune into your thoughts, your feelings. Now, at last I can be in your arms, in your heart. I've only caught fleeting pictures of you. If you were by a mirror whilst I was tuned in, I would see your reflection.'

'So all that Faye tells me is true. She says that she and you are fairies'. That she sent for me.'

'It's hard to believe, I know. Faye is the one who told me where you were, how to tune into your thoughts. She said she could bring you to me. Faye's watched you for many years. I think that she's fallen in love with you Daddy.'

'I think that I love her too but everything's happened so fast, it's hard to keep pace. I came to see Sarah for a rest. Now my life is twice as complicated as it was before I left home.' Donna's face drops. 'Don't look like that. I'm glad it's turned out this way. You, my sweet little fairy, are a wonderful complication.'

'I know that it must be difficult for you Daddy. I promise I'll be no trouble. I just couldn't bear to be away from you any longer.'

'Not all complications are bad. I don't always explain myself properly. You and Faye are a good type of complication. As far as I'm concerned, I'm the luckiest man alive. Four beautiful children, a stunner of a woman in my life. Who could ask for more?'

'We are the luckiest Fairies' to have such a wonderful, loving man in our lives,' says Donna, hugging me tighter then ever. All this emotion brings my other children to mind. I realise how much fun they are. What pleasure they have given me over the years. They might be a bit untidy around the house, so what? At least they're around. My thoughts return home. I can picture us all, sitting in the garden, watching films, play-fighting. James and Peter like to gang up against me, in wrestling matches. I can't wait to be with all my children again. I'm startled by a yelp, coming from Donna.

'You've already put me in the family picture! I saw those thoughts. You really do care for me as much as the others, don't you?'

'Of course I do, sweetie. Perhaps, in some way, I've felt you all these years. Now we've got each other, the family's complete.'

'I can see why Faye's fallen for you,' says Donna. I feel myself blush.

'You're the least selfish person I've ever met.'

'No, just a man who nearly lost sight of what he had.'

Eleven.

The Not So Great Escape.

All of a sudden, there's a tremendous crashing, coming from the stairway. A woman appears in the room.

'Hi I'm Shauna.' she says to me. 'No time to shake hands. Donna, Alex, you must go quickly!' She looks worried. 'Some Council members have turned up. Donna, take your father to Fred's house, we think they're looking for you.'

'How? No one else knows about the meeting.' Donna is frightened. 'How could they know?'

'We'll find that out later, there's no time for questions now, just leave! Wait for us to contact you,' says Shauna. 'We'll try and keep them busy until you get away. You must hurry!' Donna grabs my hand.

'Quickly, Daddy, follow me.' She's in a panic. 'This way.' There's another door that leads us out of the basement. I'd not noticed it before, it opens into some sort of tunnel. Donna drags me down the tunnel at great speed.

'This leads to an opening in the woodland just behind Faye's house. We must get to Fred's house, we'll be safe there.' When we reach the exit, Donna peeks her head out cautiously, signalling me to stay back a while.

'It's all clear, Daddy, we must get to your car.'

'Donna stop, what's the great rush? Who are these people, why are you so afraid of them?'

'They're members of The Council. We're in great danger if they find out that we've met. Faye and Shauna are in danger too. We must get to Fred Spelling's place, it's a safe house.'

'Shouldn't we go back for Faye and Shauna?' I ask. 'If they are in danger, they'll need us.'

'No Daddy, don't go back,' Donna begs. 'They're only in danger if we two are seen together. Faye can handle the situation without us. We need to get away now!'

'Sarah's car is in the lane outside. You stay here until you hear the engine running.'

'Don't leave me Daddy, I'm scared.' Donna looks like a small child. She grabs hold of me. 'I'm coming with you, I don't want to lose you again.'

'You're with me now. I won't let anything happen to you, stay low, follow me.' Very gingerly, we make our way to Sarah's car. I reach for the keys. I can't find them anywhere. They must be back at Faye's somewhere.

'Donna, I have to go back, I don't have the keys, you stay here. If anyone comes, you hide as best you can. I won't be long.' As I turn to look at Donna, she's crying, biting her bottom lip. This is exactly what Jay does when she's worried.

'Please don't cry sweetie, it'll be Ok,' I reassure her. I'll be careful. I'll be back in no time. Just stay hidden.'

'Don't let them catch you,' Donna wails. 'I want you back in one piece.' I gently pull away from her and head back to the entrance in the woods. I feel the anger welling up inside of me. Who are these people who want to keep my daughter from me? What right do they have to deprive a child her family? My blood burns, coursing through my veins. I've never known such anger. I must destroy these people. Donna's my flesh and blood, she's got the right to freedom as much as anyone else on this earth. *Calm down Alex....Why the fuck should I calm down? These people are trying to run the lives of others, they've no right....You have to calm down. You'll only mess things up if you don't keep your head. You need to think straight....OK! OK! OK! I'm composed.'* Making my way back through the tunnel, the hairs on the back of my neck are ridged. I'm overcome with a cold sweat. As I near the basement entrance, I can hear faint voices. I put my ear to the door. There is nobody in the basement. Slowly, I enter the room. I hear sounds coming from up the stairs. *Shit, where could the keys be?... They could only be in the bedroom. Oh dear God, I need you now.* Faye, Shauna and the others are in the lounge. They're talking in raised voices. I want to burst in, to defend the woman I love. But I know this would only make things worse. I make my way up the stairs to her bedroom. I search in vain. The keys are nowhere to be seen, not on the floor or the bedside table. I must have put them down in the kitchen when we got back from the pub last night. *Why didn't I try the kitchen first?* Again, I tackle the stairs as quietly as I can. The raised voices are still coming from the lounge.

'Who's this Alex person? How do you know him?' It's John's voice. I knew he was following me. All the questions in the pub the other night. For the first time in my life, I felt an anger so strong, I wanted to kill. *Get Donna away first. You can come back once she's safe....It might be too late then. What if Faye and Shauna are hurt before I get back?...You heard Donna, she said Faye can look after herself....I swear if any harm comes to Faye, I'll not rest untill those responsible are lying dead at my feet....You are losing it again, try to stay focussed on getting Donna away.* I move away from the lounge and into the kitchen. The keys are on the side by the sink. *Thank you God.* I grab them, sneak out the front door and make a dash for the car. Donna is on the ground by the car, shaking.

'It's Ok darling, told you I wouldn't be long.' I lift her up off the ground, open the car door. 'Come on, get in, we'll soon be away from here.' Donna slides over to the passenger side. We scream away like the proverbial bat out of hell.

'Why Fred Spelling's house? Don't tell me he's a fairy as well!'

'No, Fred's not a fairy but he's a very powerful man. He sympathises with our plight.'

'How do you mean 'powerful'? Fred's got to be in his seventies.'

'Don't be fooled by his age. Fred's the only human who can protect us. We'll be safe with him, he's helped us get this far.'

'This is all beyond me, Donna. The biggest adventure I've had, is riding my bike at night without the lights on! I'm not the James Bond, type!'

'Well, Daddy, today you are my hero! Who needs Bond?' *If my children could see me now, I wonder what they'd have to say.* I picture myself as a super hero. Saving my children from all sorts of troubles.

'Daddy! Keep your eyes on the road, you'll have us in a ditch if you're not careful!' Donna wakes me from my daydreaming.

'Sorry, sweetie, I was just thinking about your sister and brothers. I wonder what they'd make of all this. They already think I'm a borderline nutcase.'

'My sister and brothers,' Donna gives an excited yelp. 'I love it when you talk about me having a sister and brothers. I can't wait to be with them! I'll show them everything that you've been shown. Then they'll know you are not nutty, just specially perceptive to the world around you. To the things that really matter in life.' What Donna says, makes me feel good about myself. We're nearing Fred's house, what's he going to think? He's only met me once and I wasn't at my best that day! Still, he did say to pop in if ever I was at a loss. I think my present situation qualifies!

'I just hope he's home, Donna. I don't want to get Sarah and Rob mixed up in this. They've got enough problems of their own at the moment.' We get out the car and run to Fred's house. I'm looking round nervously, to make sure that we've not been followed. Before we have a chance to get to the front door, it opens. Fred stands in the doorway.

'Donna, Alex, come in quickly, I have been expecting you,' Fred says, with a welcoming smile.

Twelve.

A Generous Host.

Even though it's a warm day, there's a chill in the house. To my surprise, the house is in a modern state of decoration. I was expecting it to be furnished like my late Grandmother's home. An old clock on the mantle, ticking away the seconds of boredom. Newspapers on the chair in the bay. A big onyx table-lighter. No, this place looks like a young city couple live here, not a salty old sea dog. No souvenirs from Fred's travels round the world. Just a beautiful home that any city slicker would be proud of.

'Wow, this place is great, Fred! Who does the decorating?'

'I do, of course! Wouldn't let anybody else do it for me,' beams Fred. 'Anyway, you're not here to talk about interior design. Can I take it that the meeting between you two didn't run as smoothly as we hoped?'

'Some of The Council turned up shortly after I did, so we had to make a swift getaway,' says Donna.

'I recognised one of the voices,' I chip in. 'It was John's, the grocer. I'm sure it was.'

'I didn't think it'd take him long to get involved,' glared Fred. 'He's near the top of The Council. They don't usually send him round to do the dirty work. It must be because Faye's involved. He's always had a thing for her. Be careful Alex, he wants you on two counts. The Council don't want you and Donna meeting up. John wants Faye for himself.'

'I don't think they know that we've met yet,' says Donna. 'Otherwise there'd have been more of them turn up at the house.'

'I must go back and see if Faye and Shauna are alright,' I interrupt.

'No! You stay well away,' Fred orders. 'Faye and Shauna are safe as long as The Council have no proof. If you turn up, that'll only give them cause to look deeper. Somebody must have tipped them off, but who? How do you know what John's voice sounds like Alex, have you met him?'

'Yes, he was at the pub the other night, we played darts together. He was asking lots of questions. I thought nothing of it 'til I heard him at Faye's place. He was asking Faye who I was, how she knew me.'

'Well, with a bit of luck, that's all he's interested in. It might be that he's trying to mark his territory. He may know nothing of the meeting between you two. If that's the case, the problem's not as big as we first thought.'

'It'd still be a big problem! Faye and I are in love. She wants to come with me and Donna.'

'Tangled, tangled webs,' says Fred, sighing. 'Why is

nothing ever simple? Love comes along and stirs up a heap of trouble.' I look towards Donna, she's smiling from ear to ear, ecstatic.

'You don't look like the scared, helpless child that was in my arms just minutes ago! What's brought this look of great joy to your face?'

'You have, you and Faye in love!' she squeals. 'The two people I need most in life, you're in love. Nothing could be better.'

'Don't get your hopes up too high,' cautions Fred. 'We're not out of the woods yet. We're not sure how much The Council knows. I can't see John letting Faye leave without a fight.'

'If he wants a fight, I'll give him a fight,' I shout, trying to sound brave in front of Donna. 'I've been beaten up by smaller men than him before!'

'Daddy, it's no joke, John and the rest of them are extremely powerful. You don't know what you're up against.'

'Surely we have some allies, don't we? You and Faye can't be the only ones who want to lead your own lives. Can't you get all the rebels to unite, to stand up to these despots?'

'There are thousands of others but most of them are too frightened to say anything in case they're betrayed, given up to The Council.'

'Fred, where do you stand in all this? Donna says you're not a fairy. So what are you? How are you able to protect us from The Council?'

'Who am I? Alex, I'm just a simple man, like yourself. Who, many years ago, fell in love with a wonderful woman. She was a powerful fairy.'

'Did she give you a lot of electric shocks?'

'Daddy, listen. Fred's telling you something sad. And how far The Council are prepared to go to keep us apart.'

'We could only meet in secret. Many years before, when fairies' had just started to get the breeding programme right with humans. Queen Tiziana and King Orfeo decreed that The Higher Council must, at all costs, keep the secret and that only the Fairy Kingdom must know of this.'

'Stop! All this is really confusing, someone's lying. Faye told me she was one of the first human-fairy hybrids. Now, you're telling me that you met a fairy woman many years ago. I'm not happy with all this deception.'

'No one is lying to you. Fairies' age much slower than we do. The most natural, pure breeds live for five hundred years or more. None of us know how long fairy-human hybrids live but we do know that once they reach adulthood, the ageing seems to slow down markedly.'

'How long ago, was this?' I ask. A solemn expression appears on Fred's face.

'After knowing Sophie for quite some time. She told me she was fifty years old. Like you, I couldn't take it all in. I was in my mid-twenties, yet Sophie looked younger than me. I only really started to believe the things I'd been shown, many years into our relationship. I'd left it too late.' Tears fill Fred's eyes. 'Sophie vanished before I had a chance to tell her that I was now able to open my mind to all the wonderous things our future would hold. You're now being given the chance to have two very special people in your life. I beg you Alex, don't lose that chance like I did.' Fred is overcome. Donna moves over to comfort him. Putting her arm around his shoulder.

'It's OK Fred, you don't have to say any more. I know it must be hard.' Wiping the tears from his eyes, with a handkerchief, Fred continues.

'Just a week before Sophie disappeared, she gave me an amulet. She said I was to "Wear it all the times, never take it off." She must have known something was about to happen, she had foreseen her disappearance or known that we had been found out. She must have known that we were in danger. I thought that the amulet was a token of her love for me but it's much more than that. It has deep, powerful protection spells woven into it. As long as I have this....,' Fred pulls the amulet from under his shirt. It's a simple looking, round, gold, disk with a turquoise stone simply inset. It hangs from a finely crafted gold lanyard. Radiating from the edges of the stone is a shimmering light. 'I can't be harmed by any members of The Council. Alex, you must take this now,' says Fred. 'I'm done with it, I don't think that I have many years left in me. It's someone else's turn to take on the fight. Fate seems to have chosen you.'

'Me, I don't think I'm your man! I was beaten up by girl guides.'

'Daddy, don't lie. I know how brave you are, you'd give your last breath for a just cause.' Donna has more faith in me than I have in myself.

'I don't know how to fight. If all you say is true. How can I fight against The Council? You say they're very powerful.' I don't want Donna to think too badly of me but I have to be realistic.

'Once you accept this amulet, you'll see just how strong you can be,' Fred assures me. 'It has given me great powers, great understanding, over the years. Donna and

Faye need you to be strong for them. They deserve the chance to live their lives in a way that will make them happy. Throughout history people have been held back through fear and ignorance. We can't continue that cycle. It's time to evolve a better understanding. Despite all their powers, their claims to be the enlightened ones. The Council cower like a lamb in a lion's den. They gave the go-ahead for the mixed breeding programme. Now they have to deal with the consequences of their actions.' Fred's face is burning red with anger. 'I'm sorry to rant but if The Fairy Council had come out into the open, then maybe Sophie and I would have had many wonderful love filled years together. I implore you Alex, don't let them do the same to you, to the ones you love.' Wow! I see what Donna meant when she said Fred's a powerful man. The passion of his speech made the hairs on the back of my neck stand on end.

'I can't take the amulet. It was Sophie's gift to you. You must never take it off, you'd be putting yourself in danger,' I protest.

'What danger can I be in at this time of life? What could they take from me? I have what, five years left in me, that's being optimistic. I need you to take over the battle. You can give us hope for the future. This is your chance to make a difference, not just today but for generations to come.'

'Daddy, please take the amulet, it's our only chance to be a whole family. It'll give you the strength and protection you're going to need to keep us together,' Donna is almost begging. 'I have waited so long to be with you and my sister and brothers.' The anger is building in me. Anger at those that want to keep us apart. No one is going to take my daughter away from me. I have already missed so much of her growing up. I'd do the same for Jay, James and Peter. I came on holiday for a rest but found a daughter, a girlfriend and a crusade. Sounds just like me, nothing I plan ever turns out the way I expect. Fred is holding out the amulet, offering it to me. I hesitate for a moment, then looking into Donna's eyes. I take hold of the amulet. It was like being hit by lightning. A surge of energy ran through me. So this is satori, I understand now. I feel twenty years younger.

'Holy shit.'

'I knew you'd take it, Daddy,' says Donna, proudly. 'You are the man I felt you to be for all these years. We can do it, Daddy. You, Faye, me, the rest of our family, we can take on The Council and win!'

'Hey, slow down. You're staying way out of harm's way. You must stay with Fred until we find out what's going on. I must go and see if Faye and Shauna are alright, find out what The Council know.'

'No, Alex, I'll go. Your going, would only cause John to look closer at Faye's movements. If I go, I won't be a threat to his ego. You stay here with Donna, until I find out what's going on.'

'You'd best take your amulet back for the time being. You'll need its protection', I say, offering it to Fred.

'I can't take it back. Once it's been passed on, the previous holder may never take it back', insists Fred. 'That is why you must take extreme care of it. It will only do good in good hands. The amulet cannot be used for bad or for evil deeds. In the hands of the wrong person, it will become redundant and you can't let that happen. I'll be Ok. I'll just take some vegetables round with me on the pretext that Faye had asked me to.'

'If John's still there, causing trouble. Make sure you bludgeon him to death with a marrow! How will we know if we're in the clear?'

'I'll contact the two of you as soon as it's safe.' With that, Fred leaves.

'Don't worry, daddy, not all the power of the amulet has left him. Fred gave it away in good faith, for the right reason. He has been left with a lot of protective powers, he'll come to no harm.'

Thirteen.

The Waiting Game.

Donna and I are left on our own. This morning, when I woke. I had no idea she even existed. Now I have a new daughter whom I love dearly, yet I know nothing about her, or her mother.

'Donna, where does your mother stand on all this? Is she on your side? Did she want you to meet me?'

'I've never met my mother. I've never felt my mother. I can only assume that she's disappeared as well,' Donna replies softly. 'I've felt you all my life but have never had the same feelings about her. I wish I had. At least then I would know that she's still alive, that I would have the chance of meeting her one day.'

'Why are The Fairy Council so against you mixing with humans. After all they were quick enough to steal our genes? We have unwittingly saved their species. Don't they owe us something in return?"

'They've lived alongside the human race for thousands of years. They see how you treat each other, how you persecute those who are different from yourselves. Humans can't seem to accept members of their own race if they have different colour skin or worship a different God. How could they accept a new race, when they can't accept themselves?"

'Not every human is like that Donna, you know that. Otherwise you wouldn't want to be with us. Hiding is not the answer, it will only lead to trouble. You have said that there are thousands of human-fairy hybrids who want to mix freely. If the lid is kept on, one day the pot will explode. It seems to me it's at boiling point right now. Can't they see they're acting in the same way as humans act. Actions they claim to despise, yet they're using to suit themselves.'

'You don't have to convince me. I want my freedom. I want to be able to choose who I love. I hate all this hiding. I'm as much human as fairy. I want to keep both sides of my roots. I've lost my mother, been kept from you. Fred has lost the only woman he has ever loved. They'll try to keep Faye apart from you.' I can't help but smile. Donna looks the image of Jay when she's on her high horse.

'It's not funny, Daddy.'

'I'm sorry, sweetie, I'm not laughing at you. It's just that you reminded me of Jay. You can both be fierce when you get angry.'

'Well, we must get that from you. I've felt you get angry in the past, it's quite frightening. I must admit though, over the last couple of years. I've not felt much anger or happiness at all from you. It felt that you had lost all your emotions. What has caused you to stop caring about yourself?'

'That's a long story. I haven't stopped caring about me. I just seem to have lost my zest for life. Don't worry, it'll come back with a vengeance, one of these days.'

'We'll be Ok once we get away from here,' sighs Donna. 'I can't wait, I just want to lead an open life.'

'I'm not sure that's true sweetie, it might be just coincidence. Before I left to come down here, I had a run-in with a policeman. In fact, two run-ins in the space of twelve hours. I don't think that it's my imagination, this policeman looked just like John. Is it possible that this policeman could be connected in some way?'

'Oh, Daddy, it could be a coincidence but I think that's unlikely. What were the run-ins about?'

'Well, the first was to do with a report from one of my neighbours. I'd seen a fairy at my window so I went into the garden to look for her. The second was the next morning when I was driving down here. I was stopped by one of the policemen from the night before for having a faulty brake light.'

'The fairy you saw was not a real fairy but a projection from Faye. She put a guardian spell around the projection so it would not be detected. If this policeman is connected, then the projection must have leaked somehow. I don't know how. Faye's spells have never had any leaks in them before. The Council must be getting worried. If they did tap into Faye's spell they are using some powerful magic indeed. You must be right about the pot, ready to explode.'

'Why do you and Faye say that Faith is not real. She must be real, I had a picnic with her.'

'Where did you have a picnic.'

'In the New Forest, when I was driving down here.'

'You can't have. She has no physical presence.'

'Yes she does, she kissed me and I got a static shock from her.'

'Daddy, that's impossible. Projections can't touch you. Something's gone wrong. We must let Faye know there's a chance her spells are leaking. If the leaks are not plugged, we may as well advertise our plans in the national press! I'm scared, Daddy.'

'What should we do?' I ask. 'Should we wait to hear from Fred, or should we go to Faye now?'

'Fred, said we were to wait. I'm inclined to agree with what you're thinking, that we should go to Faye's. If you wait in the car when we get there, I'll check to see if the coast's clear. Faye needs to know about her spells as soon as possible. If her guard is down, just for a split second, the consequences could be disastrous.'

'Your knowing what I'm thinking and feeling, it is going to take a lot of getting used to. I'll have to be so careful what I think about in future, I don't want you thinking me a strange person.'

'You are a strange person, Daddy, strange and wonderful! You worry about others more than you need. That's the only strange thing about you. Look how you're worried about Faye and Shauna now and you hardly know them. When we are all together, I won't need to read your thoughts and feelings to find out about you, or how you are. Because I'll be with you. I promise I'll not read your private thoughts. I only tapped in because I wanted to get to know you.'

'When we get through this, we'll have all the time in the

world to get to know each other. You have a whole family to get to know, not just a sister and brothers. But your aunt Sarah and uncle Rob, your Grandmother.'

'Then I pray to God that we get through this. To be with my family is all I've ever wanted.'

'Come on then, sweetie, let's get the ball rolling, time for action. The waiting game's over. Donna and I jump in the car and speed to Faye's house.

Fourteen.

Spell Binding.

We screech to a stop, tyres turning to smoke. Donna hardly waits for the car to stop before she's out, rushing to Faye's front door.

'Stay here Daddy, I'll let you know if it's safe for you to come in.' I can feel the adrenalin rush, racing through my body. I haven't felt this scared or alive for a long time. I'm not a violent man but, right at this moment I'm bursting for a fight. The Amulet seems to have awoken something within. The anger of the past two or three years. The years since Charlie and me split up, is pushing its way to my head like the molten magma of an untamed volcano. I can no longer pretend that nothing hurts me, that I'm coping. I can wait no longer. I storm towards Faye's front door, with images of Faye and Donna being bullied by John and whoever else turned up with him. I bang on the door with the thunder of a thousand storms. *What if they are being hurt by John?* Stepping back two paces, I charge at the door, striking it first with my shoulder. The door explodes off its hinges. I end up flat on my face on top of the door. I look up to see Shauna, Faye, Donna and Fred looking down at me in disbelief.

'What the hell do you think you're up to?' shouts Faye.

'I've come to save you,' I jump to my feet. 'Where are they? You're safe now.'

'Alex, they've gone,' Faye answers. 'What did you say to John about me the other night?'

'I don't know, I hardly mentioned you, I was too busy losing at darts.'

'You must have said something. He seemed to think that you were totally besotted with me.'

'I might have mentioned that I'd met you, that I thought you were the prettiest woman I've ever met.' Faye looks at Fred.

'Have you given him the Amulet Fred?'

'I thought that he'd need it more than I do. I can fight no longer. It's time someone else had a go.'

'Fred, you should know better than that. Alex's not ready to deal with the power of the Amulet. As my front door can bare witness.'

'He's as ready as I was, when it was given to me. What harm can it do?'

'If Alex starts running around like a lunatic, thinking he can save the world. It can do a lot of harm.' Shauna says to Fred.

'Daddy's not a lunatic,' protests Donna.

'Sorry, I didn't mean it to come out that way. The Amulet

can change a person, if they are unable to control the power.'

'Alex, John has no idea about you and Donna meeting,' Says Faye. 'He came around because he's a jealous man. He tried talking me out of having anything to do with you. Had you burst in five minutes ago, you'd have given the game away. John would have seen you and Donna together. You can't just rush in and play the hero. The Amulet is a most powerful weapon. You're not ready for it. Fred, you were with Sophie for many years before she gave it to you. That's because humans need to be in its presence a long time before they can cope with the amulet's guardianship.'

'It'll be aright Faye,' I say. 'I won't let the power go to my head.'

'It's too late now. You have it, you will have to keep it. From now on, you must not just think twice before you attempt any heroics. Think three or four times, then think again!' Faye turns to Donna and Shauna, 'Hold on to your hats girls, Fred has just released a tornado.' Talking to all of us, Faye says. 'Donna tells me she thinks that my spells might be leaking. We must bind any holes that have appeared. Shauna, Donna, I'm going to have to call upon you to help me. We must combine our magic to plug the leak. Alex, we're also going to need the presence of the Amulet. I'm afraid that means you too. You must do nothing. Any feelings and thoughts you get, please, please, please don't act upon them.'

'I thought you said John knows nothing of Donna and me. So why do you need a spell?'

'He seems not to know but we can't take a chance. From what Donna has told me, someone knows something about me getting you down here. Better to be safe than sorry. Don't worry, the spell's not dangerous.'

'I'm fine. I feel stronger and more in control than I have for years.'

'You're stronger but you are certainly not in control, please take my word for it. During the incantations, you must stay still, keep quiet. With the grace of God, we'll be able to mend my abilities without further damage.'

'Please don't be too hard on him,' Donna pleads. 'Daddy didn't know he wasn't ready for the Amulet, Fred and me pushed him into taking it. I didn't even know the dangers.' It's so nice to have Donna come to my rescue. I'm aware though, that Faye's not angry with me.

'Will you be needing me?' Fred enquires. 'Or can I go home and put my feet up?'

'Could you stay until we've finished?' asks Faye. 'Keep a look-out, in case any Council members come back. If my spells are leaking, we must assume that until they're fixed it's not safe to leave anything to chance.'

'And put the kettle on while you're there. I could murder a cup of tea,' says Shauna.

'No sugar for me,' Donna chips in. The four of us make our way down to the basement. Fred stays in the kitchen. Faye moves a small table to the centre of the room and places a cushion at each side. There's a large black bowl in the centre of the table.

'Alex, you sit there, remember, say and do nothing. I'm sorry to be so hard on you. I realise you have the Amulet through no fault of your own but until you learn to control the power it holds and which it has given to you, we must be careful.' Faye's voice is a lot calmer now. As Donna and Shauna sit, Shauna winks at me and smiles. For some silly reason, I picture Shauna naked.

'Alex!, Daddy!' Yell Faye and Donna, disapprovingly.

'Sorry, I didn't mean to think that.' Shauna looks at me and giggles. Faye rummages through some drawers and shelves. I've still not quite calmed down. I'm shaking from the adrenalin rush. I was ready for a fight but, alas, it wasn't meant to be. Both Donna and Shauna reach into small purses. They take out some kind of flowers, they place the flowers into the bowl on the table. Without anyone touching them, the flowers start to smoke. I look to Donna, shocked at what I see. Her captivating blue eyes have turned completely white, she has no pupils. A cold shudder runs down my spine. I look to Shauna, her eyes are the same. *Is this what's supposed to happen?...What if something's wrong?...Should I bring this to Faye's attention?...No, remember what Faye said, no matter what, do or say nothing.* Faye turns around, walks towards the table and sits at the opposite end. Her eyes are white as well. She places something in the bowl. I can't make out what it is. As Faye's hand moves away from the bowl, a blue mist decends upon us. We're fully emerged in the mist. I can hear the thoughts of the three of them but it's not clear, as their thoughts are all jumbled together. I can even hear my thoughts coming back to me. This is the strangest feeling. I'm no longer Alex. I'm all four of us and they are me! I become aware of the Amulet hanging around my neck. It's tingling. I have the urge to take it off.

'Leave the Amulet. ' I'm not sure if this was spoken or a thought.

'Resist the temptation to remove it.' Donna and Shauna link hands with both myself and Faye. The three of them start to chant.

'Powers close in
Powers far out
Hear us plead
Hear us shout
There are holes in the weave
There are holes in the weft
If all escapes
We'll have no powers left

We ask not for one
But for all that are here
Please send us a patch
Let it adhere

If, your ears are hearing
If, your eyes are wide
This net that is leaking
Put a stich in its side

Powers close in
Powers far out
Hear us plead
Hear us shout.'

The room fills with bright blue electrical sparks and swirls of smoke. A powerful wind enters the basement. I feel I'm going to be torn from the floor. Donna's and Shauna's grip on my hands tighten, their nails dig into me. I try to pull away but my hands are locked. *Fuck! These girls are strong.* CRACK! There is a bolt of lightning. It strikes the bowl in the middle of the table, exploding it into dust. Then not a sound, not a spark, just the sound of gentle breathing.

I'm exhausted, the others look the same. None of us speak for quite some time. We just sit looking at each other. I'm wondering if this is the end or is there more to come.

'That's it, Alex,' says Faye. 'The magic's done. Oh, and you've done well for a first timer.'

'I did nothing, I just sat and watched. I must admit you three did look a bit freaky with the white eyes. I'm glad they're back to the right colour.'

'The eyes turn white for clear vision. Yours were the same,' Shauna informs me. I notice that the bowl on the table is in one piece, I'm sure it was blown apart. Pointing to the bowl in the centre of the table. I ask.

'How can that be? I saw that bowl smashed by the lightning.'

'No, you saw its essence blown apart, to release the spell. Good magic destroys nothing good in the physical world.'

'So what do we do now? Are we safe to see each other in open? Can Donna and I have a normal father daughter relationship?'

'We are far from safe. The spell we just performed was to stop any leaks from now on, nothing else. We still don't know how much The Council are aware of. Our next job is to find out,' Says Faye.

'How are we going to do that?' Shauna asks.

'I'm going to have to pretend to listen to John. I'll go to see him this evening. I'll tell him I decided not to see Alex anymore, that he's going back home in a strop. This'll give you a chance to get Donna away from here, Alex.'

'What, you mean that I have to leave? What am I going to tell Sarah and Rob? They expected me to stay at least a fortnight.'

'You'll just have to make up a convincing story for your

sudden departure. Say you're missing your children.'

'I have an idea, Daddy, when was the last time either Sarah or Rob saw Jay?'

'I don't know, two maybe three years ago, why?'

'Well, you said I look just like Jay. If I come back to Sarah's with you, we can pretend I'm Jay. We can say there's some problem at home that only you can sort out.'

'I suppose it could work. Will you be able to answer any questions, if your aunt Sarah asks about the family?'

'Don't forget that I've been tuning into you and yours' Donna pauses, 'I mean ours, for most of my life. I think I've enough knowledge to fake it for a couple of hours.'

'That's your side of the plan worked out. As for me and Shauna, we'll go to see John at six o'clock this evening, that's when he shuts the shop. I'll tell him he was right, you did turn out to be a waste of space. That I told you to sling your hook. If you and Donna go back to Sarah's now and get your things ready to leave. You must not try to leave 'til six, you'll be safe with John out of the way, comforting me.'

'What about you? I thought you wanted to come with us? I'm not going to leave you in the hands of that creep.' I'm worried Faye won't come along.

'I do want to come but the important thing is to get Donna safely away and home with you. I can come to you a little later, when we're sure that The Council don't suspect. I'll join you, I promise, just give me a couple of weeks to clear things up here.'

'A couple of weeks!' I protest. 'How can I be sure that you'll be safe, what if The Council already know what's going on. What if they're waiting for us to make the first move?'

'Alex, we have no choice. If they do know, then it's a battle that we're going to have to fight. You'll be safe as long you have the Amulet. It'll keep you and Donna from harm. As for me, I'm stronger than I look. I think my powers can match anything they can throw at me. Once you're gone, don't try to contact me. I'll keep in touch through Sarah. She need not know the truth. Only that you and I are in love, that I want to come a see you soon.'
An excited yelp comes from Donna.

'You're in love! Everything's falling into place.' Donna's like a small child, I wonder if she relises that things don't always run to plan.

'What if The Council don't let you leave, what if you disappear like Sophie and Donna's mother? I can't bear the thought of not seeing you again.'

'I've a few tricks up my sleeve, I don't intend to vanish into thin air. John is a man. Most men are weak when it comes to a woman oozing out charm. If I have my way I'll charm him into non-existence.' I gather, from this remark, Faye despises John as much as I do.

'What are you going to do, Shauna?' I ask. 'How are you going to come through this unscathed?'

'I'll just have to come to live with you as well. I hope you have bunk beds.'

'You're more than welcome to stay, we'll need axel grease and a shoe horn to get us into the house. It's lucky none of us are very big.'

'I was kidding. I had plans to move away from here anyway,' says Shauna. 'Just you worry about Donna and yourself at the moment. I've friends that'll be only too glad for me to stay with them.'

'Well, don't forget if you get into trouble, you can always

give me a call.' I'm feeling strong, protective. 'Now that I have the Amulet, I can protect us all.'

'Alex, slow down, you have no idea about the kind of the power you have or how to wield it,' says Faye.

'Don't search for your new abilities,' says Shauna. 'Let them grow in you. Anyway, it's about time you and Donna to got going.' I don't want to leave, I hope this is not the last time I see Faye. I am torn between getting Donna away and staying back to fight John face-to-face.

'Don't even think about it!' Faye shouts. 'We can take care of John far better than you, trust me. He's not going to know what hit him, by the time Shauna and I've finished with him.'

'Will you please stop reading my thoughts?' It's not fair that you know everything that I'm planning. You must promise not to read me, unless it's really necessary.'

'I promise, just get out of here!' Faye snaps. 'I'll contact you through Sarah as soon as I can. Alex, don't forget that I love you.'

'I love you too.' I feel myself welling up. 'Come on sweetie, it's time to meet your other family,' I say to Donna. I walk over to Faye, hug her tight to me, Donna and Shauna join us.

'Ouch, that's the most painful group hug I've ever had. Remind me to buy a rubber suit as soon as we get home!' Shauna, looks at me and laughs.

'You sure that you haven't already got one.'

'One more thing before I go, it's a big thing to ask but I've got to ask it. Sarah and Rob: they're unable to have children. Is there anything that you could do to give them a child. A way in which it seems to them that they've conceived naturally?'

'Anything else whilst we are at it, a pot of gold maybe?'
Shauna laughs. 'Don't you think we've got enough on our
plates?'

'I know this is not the best of times but you're the only
ones who can help. It's so important that I take this
opportunity, this is Rob and Sarah's last chance.'

'We'll try our best,' beams Faye. 'Now go!'

Fifteen.

Eat, Drink and Be Merry.

Donna and I walk to the car. We are both aware that we are walking into the unknown, what lies around the corner is anyone's guess.

'Are you scared Daddy?' she asks, biting her lip, nervously.

'A little, this is something that we have to do though.'

'You can just walk away, not involve yourself further. Go home, forget all that has happened.'

'How can I do that? You're my baby, I'll try to do my best for you as I would for your sister and brothers. Donna, I've not known you long. But I do love you.'

'No wonder Faye loves you Daddy. No wonder I love you. You really do care.'

'Stop, you're embarrassing me, I'm no different to most parents in the world. It's human nature to protect your children.' We get in the car and head for Sarah's. I wonder if Sarah will notice that Donna is not Jay?

'Will Sarah be home?'

'No, she and Rob are still at work, that will give us time to run through any answers you might need. What you, as Jay, have been doing with your life.'

'How's everybody going to take it when we get home, the fact that you have another daughter?'

'Your guess is as good as mine, sweetie. Our family is pretty open minded. You'll be made welcome from the moment they meet you. I'll get some stick for not telling anyone about you all these years. If I say I didn't know about you 'til now, they'll have a go at me for that. I'll be in for a bit of a grilling, I can cope with that. As long as we know the truth, if we share that with Jay, James and Peter, that's all that really matters.' We reach Sarah's house, this time I have the key. As we walk into the house. Donna's face drops.

'Oh Daddy, the feelings in this house, all that love mixed with sadness.'

'That's why I asked Faye and Shauna to help. Your aunt and uncle are devoted to each other. A child of their own would complete the story.'

'Well, let's pray that Faye and Shauna can do something for them.'

'I'm going to sort out my clothing and pack my bag. I think Sarah's going to be disappointed to find out I'm leaving so soon.'

'We can come back, when this is all over Daddy, we could make it a family holiday, the five of us.'

'You're really getting into this family business. I can't imagine what the reaction of your sister and brothers is going to be like. The months ahead are going to be full, to say the least.' Donna starts jumping up and down with excitement. She grabs hold of me. We dance around the house, laughing, singing like a pair of idiots. Donna's still very much a child, we collapse on to the sofa, laughing.

'I'm so happy Daddy! Faye promised me this, she's come through for me! You don't need to be concerned about John so much. I'm beginning to belive that Faye gets anything she sets out to get.'

'Come, let's get things sorted before aunt Sarah and uncle Rob get home. I want to spend a little time with them before we go.'

After my things are packed, Donna suggests we cook dinner for Sarah and Rob.

'We could all have a chat over the meal,' she says.

'Let's see what they have in the fridge. I can cook a great spaghetti Bolognese, if you can find some minced beef.'

'I can't eat beef. Do you know how to cook a vegetarian dish?'

'Is that a fairy thing too, no meat?'

'Well, that's not strictly true. This might make you feel a little queasy. I do get the urge to eat the odd woodlice and beetle. Most true fairies are insectivores.'

'You're joking with me. Aren't you?'

'Sorry, Daddy, it's no different from you eating mammals. Our digestion can't handle mammal meat. Anyway, mostly, I just eat fruit or vegetables. Bugs are just a treat on special occasions.'

'I had a cousin when I was younger, he'd eat bees and worms. I wonder, do you think that he's a fairy hybrid too? Michael was his name, I just couldn't figure out why he never got stung by the bees as he munched away on them.'

'I've found some soya, that'll do, by the time you've made the sauce, you won't be able to tell the difference,' says Donna.

'You were joking about the bugs, weren't you?' I ask with a shudder.

'No, sorry if it offends you but insects are perfectly fine to eat and full of nutrition. They're not full of fat. With you being so worried about the size of your belly, you might want to give them a try. I have some great recipes.'

'Remind me not leave you alone in the kitchen when we get home. I'm not ready for stag beetle stroganoff.'

'That's a shame, I was really looking forward to making you a caterpillar crumble,' she chuckles.

'Does Faye eat insects? I'd hate to think I might have kissed her just after she'd eaten a spider.'

'Faye may be partial to the odd six or eight legged friend, just as I am. She's still the same Faye you fell in love with, Daddy. There's always a period of adjustment at the start of a new relationship.' I'm not sure if Donna is just teasing me or if what she's saying is true. We are nearly finished cooking, when we hear the front door open.

'That must be Sarah, are you ready?'

'I'll be Ok, Daddy. I think I've inherited your powers of invention, just be ready to come to my rescue if I start going off track.'

'Ooo! What's that lovely smell?' Sarah asks, as she walks through the door. 'And who's this lovely little girl, come here and give your auntie a big hug.' Sarah and Donna embrace.

'You've not changed one bit since I last saw you. How old are you now? You must be getting on for what, 17,18?'

'I'm 22, nearly 23.'

'Surely not, my little Jay a grown woman, where has all the time gone? It seems only yesterday when your Dad phoned me to say he'd just become a daddy.'

'Tell me about it, Jay makes me feel really old. She's buying her own home now. She's earning a lot more than I was before I left my job.' I'm hoping Donna's picking up on some of this information.

'Well, it's a nice surprise to see you, Jay. Your dad didn't tell us you were coming. Have you come to stay as well?'

'I'd love to aunt Sarah, I'm afraid I've come to take Dad away. Peter's grandfather has been taken ill. So his mother's gone to stay with him for a while. She's asked if we can look after Peter.'

'Oh, Alex does that mean you're going already?' Sarah's face drops. 'You've only just got here.'

'I'm sorry sis, I can come back to see you once Dawn is back from her father's, I promise.'

'When do you have to leave? Rob's going to be upset to see you go so soon. What about Faye? She'll be disappointed too.'

'We can stay for dinner, I'm not going without saying goodbye to Rob. I've already phoned Faye to tell her. We're going to keep in touch. I wish I could've stayed as long as I had planned, I've loved seeing you again.'

'Shall I set the table?' asks Donna. She wants to give Sarah and me some time alone. Donna leaves the room.

'Well, that was a short visit, Alex.' Sarah gives me a hug. 'What am I going to do? Things are so strained between Rob and me. As much as we love each other, I can't help but think we're drifting apart. Your being here helped. We could focus on someone else for a change.'

'That's not always the answer sis, sometimes you have to look at the situation you're in, make the most of what you have. You and Rob have a strong relationship. One day you're going to look back and see just how great you two are together.'

'Must you go? Can't Peter come and stay with you here?'

'I can't take Peter out of school. He's in his last two years, everything he does now counts towards his GCSE results. We'll be back before you know it. Perhaps we could all go away together, rent a holiday cottage for a couple of weeks? How does France grab you? We used to love the French countryside. Remember Madrec, the holiday cottage in the middle of that corn field. Fresh picked corn, hot bread, with a good bottle of wine. We could go there again.'

'I must admit that sounds good to me. We could pretend we're young again. Running through the fields, playing, picnics,' Sarah smiles as she reminisces.

'Hello you two,' says Rob, as he enters through the front door. 'You both look extremely happy with yourselves.' Sarah walks over to Rob and takes him in her arms.

'Did you have a good day at work?'

'Not bad, dinner smells nice, what is it?'

'Alex and Jay cooked us a special meal. Alex has to go home and look after Peter.'

'Jay's here, where is she?' Rob calls out. 'Where's my favourite niece, stop hiding, uncle Rob wants a cuddle.'

'Rob, Jay's twenty two, she might be too old for a cuddle.' Sarah tells him.

'You're joking, twenty two, when did that happen? My little fairy, all grown up.' My heart skipped a beat, then I remembered, Rob always said that Jay looked like a fairy. He would always call James, "pixie boy."

'Uncle Rob!' squeals Donna, as she runs in the room. God, this girl is a good actor.

'So you've come to take your dad away from us, have you? You haven't altered in the slightest, well except, are you wearing contact lenses?'

'Yes, you're the first to notice, they're tinted a little as I didn't inherit Daddy's bright eyes. Dinner's ready, so if you would all care to join me in the dining room.'

'I'll just have a quick freshen up. Two ticks.' says Rob. Donna leads Sarah and me into the dining room. She's set the table stylishly, with a centre piece of flowers. At each place setting, there is a napkin and a crystal wine glass. How did Donna know where to find everything?

'This looks wonderful Jay,' Sarah says, with delight. 'I didn't realise that we had such nice things. Rob, look at this, we're eating at the "Hilton" tonight.' Donna blushes over all the attention her efforts have received. We all sit to eat. Rob cracks open a bottle of wine, he fills everyone's glass.

'A toast, please raise your glasses to my wife, Sarah, one in a million.'

'Sarah, one in a million,' we echo.

'My turn,' says Sarah. 'To my husband Rob, one in my life.'

'Rob, one in our life.'

'Your turn Alex. I think I know who he'll toast,' says Sarah.

'Ladies and gentlemen, please be up-standing, Faye, one I just met.'

'Faye, one he just met.'

'Jay please take the floor,' Rob gestures.

'Please raise your glasses to, Our family, One truly nutty family.' says Donna.

'Our family, One truly nutty family.'   After much laughter and slurping of wine, we start our meal.

'This is really tasty, who made the sauce?' asks Sarah. 'Can I have the recipe?'

'I'm afraid this is the only meal I can cook, most of my culinary efforts end up in the bin or in the cat. Thank God for the microwave. Mind you, I've been eating well since Jay moved in. You're a fantastic cook aren't you, sweetie? I'm going to miss that, when you move into your new flat.'

'Your mother was always a good cook, from what I remember,' Rob adds. 'How is she?' Donna shoots me a quick look. She's panicking, she knows nothing of Jay's mother.

'Leslie's going to be in Spain for at least another year, isn't that right sweetie,' I butt in.   'Still being super successful with each business she sets up.'

'Yes, I spoke to her the other day,' Donna says. 'She wants James and me to go over for a short break soon.'

'That should be nice, when was the last time you saw her?' asks Sarah.

'We went over last summer, for two weeks. Shortly after she bought another property that she wanted to show off.' This girl is a natural. Even I'm believing what she says.

'Did your dad tell you? he's met a new woman down here. She's a good friend of mine,' says Sarah.

'Yes, you did mention her, didn't you Daddy?   They sounded very lovey dovey on the phone earlier.'

'Your father is the first man I've known to interest Faye at all. You really must meet her before you go.'

'No! I mean, when I phoned Faye, she said that she had to go somewhere with Shauna.' Now it's my turn to panic. 'Faye can meet everyone when she comes to stay in a couple of weeks. What's the time? I think we should make a move soon.'

'Why the rush? It's only half past five, give it another hour, the roads will be much clearer by then,' says Rob.

'Coffee anyone? You can help me Daddy.' Donna and I go into the kitchen.

'That was close Daddy. I was running out of things to say about Jay's mother. What else do I need to know?'

'You're doing fine sweetie, if we just change the subject. I hate telling lies to them. I just don't want them involved, they've enough troubles of their own at the moment.'

'We're not really lying Daddy, we're just shielding them from the truth. The less they know, the better.' I carry the tray of coffees in. Sarah and Rob are chatting and laughing.

'What are you two so jovial about?'

'Oh, we're just talking about Faye, coming to see you. This sounds serious,' says Sarah. 'I've never known Faye be so keen on somebody. I told you, if you would just be yourself, you'd be Ok.'

'I think she's great. You were right, Faye's so natural, fun to be with.'

'So much fun, in fact, that you didn't come home last night! We did wonder where you'd got to. I had to catch the bus to work today,' Sarah teased.

'I'm so sorry. I forgot I had your car.' I take the keys out my pocket and give them to her. 'You could have used my car.'

'I would have but I couldn't find the keys, you really

should get a mobile phone Alex. Then I would be able to contact you.'

'Can't cope with them. People phoning at all times of the day. It's unnatural.'

'Well I would have been able to phone you to ask where your car keys were.'

'Oops, I had them with me too. Sorry that was thoughtless.'

'Lucky there's a bus that we can use' says Rob, with a smile.

'That reminds me, I hope my car starts alright, it's reluctant to start when I've not given it a go for a couple of days.'

'We've got some jump leads if it needs a bit of a boost. Are they still in the boot, Sarah?'

'I should think so, I don't think I've ever used them.'

'Well, I suppose we should be off. Donna, I'll just get my bags.'

'Who, what did you call her?' asks Sarah.

'What?' I realise my mistake.

'I thought you called Jay, Donna.'

'No, I said, dunna ye get ma bags,' I say, in my Scottish accent, that doesn't sound at all Scottish.

'Right,' says Sarah. Looking towards Rob and shrugging.

'Well sis, this is goodbye, I'll be back soon. Sorry I've had to leave without much notice.' We hug tightly. 'You're going to be fine, sweetie.' Sarah pulls away and smiles. I turn to Rob.

'It's been great to see you again Rob.' We shake hands and embrace.

'Don't leave it so long next time,' says Rob. Donna hugs Sarah and Rob.

'See you soon aunt Sarah, uncle Rob. We'll bring James and Peter next time. Tell this Faye woman I'm looking forward to meeting her, I want to make sure she's good enough for my Daddy.'

'You'll love her, I promise,' says Sarah. 'You already have one thing in common. I get static shocks from both of you!' Donna and I look at each other.

We get in the car. Sarah and Rob wait at the door to see us off.

'Please start,' I say to my car. I turn the key, it starts first time, it never does that. I turn to Donna.

'Did you do that?'

'Just a little spark in the right place,' she says, with a wink. As we pull away, we wave to Rob and Sarah.

'I do hope they're going to be alright. I hope Faye and Shauna can weave some magic for them.' Donna laughs out loud. She's looking at me as if she thinks I'm stupid.

'Dunna ya get ma bags.' We were doing so well up to that point.' She's still laughing. I do feel foolish. I'm laughing now.

'It was all I could think of, we got away with it. Sarah thinks I've been acting strange anyway. So that won't seem odd, coming from me.' We burst in to fits of laughter and can't stop for about a quarter of an hour. When we've calmed down, Donna says.

'I'm really going home, aren't I. I'm so nervous. What if my sister and brothers don't like me?'

'It's going to be strange at first, we can't get away from that. They'll love you, what's not to love? You're so much like Jay. You're no different from Peter. He's Jay and James's half brother, they all get on well.'

Sixteen.

Fly Away Home.

As I'm driving along, I realise that I don't know where I am going.

'Donna, what's the best way to the main drag?'

'Head for Lostwithiel, then cut across to Bodmin. Get onto the A30.'

'I must admit, it's a lot prettier down here than it is in Southampton. I do hope you're going to be able to cope with city life.'

'Don't worry about me Daddy, I'm a modern girl. I'm really looking forward to living in a place that doesn't close down over the winter months.'

'St Austell's not that bad, is it? Sarah says she wouldn't live anywhere else. She and Rob love it here.'

'I suppose it's Ok, if you're a little older than me. I've been longing to get to you and the big city. Whenever I've tuned into you in the past, it seemed an exciting place to be. The shops, the night life, thousands of people my age.'

'I haven't really given it a thought. Southampton, an exciting city? I suppose when you live in a place, you take it for granted. London, now that's exciting. It's like hundreds of cities in one. You have everything you need on your doorstep, galleries, clubs, theatres, restaurants of every description, it's truly a world-class city.'

'I've only been to London, once, I loved it but I wouldn't like to live there, that would be too much of a culture shock.'

We've been driving for about half an hour, when Donna says.

'Don't be alarmed Daddy. I think that blue car has been behind us for most of the journey. I've got this strange feeling, they might be Council members.

'Shall I put my foot down, try to lose them?' Before Donna had a chance to answer, my right foot was to the floor. Wow! The acceleration was unbelievable. Donna must have done something to the engine when she added that little spark.

'Careful Daddy, these roads are very twisty, turny,' screams Donna. 'You never know what's round the next cornerrrr!' At that moment, the car takes off.

'We're flying!' I shout. 'Are you doing that?'

'No! we're not flying Daddy, you just hit that hump-back bridge at seventy miles an hour, we're crashing!' The next thing I know, we are nose first in a field, with steam and smoke billowing from under what's left of the hood of the car. An acrid smell from the smoke, burns my nostrils. My eyes are stinging. How did we live through that? I turn to

Donna, she's sitting dead still, stunned.

'Are you hurt sweetie? I'm so sorry, I don't know what came over me.'

'The Amulet, that's what came over you. Faye said you must be very careful, we can't fly Daddy. I have no wings, the car certainly hasn't. Quickly, get out, we must hide. The blue car can't be far behind.' When I get out the car, Donna pulls me towards a clump of trees.

'This way, we'll hide over here.'

'Four trees is not the best of hiding places. I think the smoke signal we sent up is a clue to our whereabouts.' Then, the strangest thing I've ever seen in my life. Donna cuts a slice in the air, with her bare hands. She pulls me through the slice she's made and quickly seals it up. The world has turned into a photo negative. Everywhere I look, the colours are wrong.

'Where are we?'

'We're still in the field,' says Donna. 'But, now we're on the other side.' My heart skips.

'What do you mean, the other side?' I feel like crying. 'Did we die in the crash?'

'What? No, we didn't die. We're not on the other side of life, just the other side of Nature. Sorry, I did not mean to scare you, I forget you humans don't know this place.'

'Well, I hope they sell cigarettes this side because I left mine in the car. If I don't have one soon, I'll be a quivering jelly.'

'How can you think of smoking at a time like this?' asks Donna, in surprise. She's obviously never been a smoker.

'A time like this is when I need a smoke the most, they calm me down. I was scuba diving once and reached for my cigarettes.' Donna cups her hand around my mouth.

'Quiet!' The men from the car are looking round our crash site, they can see we're not in the car.

'Do you recognise either of them? Are they members of The Council?'

'I'm not sure Daddy, I don't know every member. I can't make out what they're saying.' There are muffled voices coming from the two men.

'If they're from The Council, won't they be able to see us?'

'No, they can come through to this side, they'd have to be lucky to guess what area we slipped into. It's very complicated, I'll explain it all to you when we have some time. There are many depths, they'd have to cut exactly the depth that I have. They can hear us though, if we're too loud, so whisper.'

'So what do we do now?'

'We wait.'

'Is it safe in here? Are there any strange beings that I should know about? You know the sort of thing, retired head masters or traffic wardens.'

'Can you not stay focussed for five seconds, Daddy? You might see some things that you're not used to, nothing will hurt you. Not all of Nature is predatory. Believe me, there are a lot of wonderful things that live on this Earth.'

'You can't blame me for being a little scared, I'm standing with my newly-acquired daughter in a Fox Talbot invention. I'm bound to be a little negative.' Donna and I stand in utter silence, watching and waiting, when something catches my eye.

'Watch out!' I scream. Donna spins around with a look of horror on her face. This look soon turns to one of relief.

'It's a rabbit, Daddy.'

'Oh yes, so it is. You have to admit, it's a big rabbit.' I've stopped shaking by this time. Looking up at us is a large albino rabbit. It has a dandelion leaf in its mouth, nose twitching. It's acting just like any other rabbit. You never know, over the last couple of days, I've come to view things in quite a different manner. Donna stoops and picks up the rabbit.

'See Daddy, he won't hurt you. He's just a fluffy wuffy wabbit, no nasty teeth or claws.'

In our distraction with the rabbit, we didn't see the men from the car, until it was too late. They were upon us. They're looking straight at me, yet they don't seem to be able to see me.

'I think that my scream may have given us away.'

'You think?' says Donna.

'Come on out, Donna. If you come back with us now, nothing will happen to you or your father,' one of the men says, standing tall and erect, full of self importance. My blood's boiling. I reach out and tear a hole in the air. Striding through the gaping hole, I make a grab for one of the men. They look shocked.

'Leave my daughter alone you bastards, if you so much as look at her I'll tear your heads off!'

'Daddy stop!' Donna tries to pull me back, I break lose. I grab a hold of the taller of the two and throw him to the ground. I follow him down. The other jumps on my back. I've never known such hatred as I'm feeling now. I rear up and throw the man from my back as if he's an insect. The first man stands up full of fury, he's huge. Charging towards me, he's holding a weapon in his hand. I can't believe my eyes, he's got a sword in his hand and it's pointing straight at me. Donna's screaming, I am too pumped up to hear what she's saying. I've only one thing on my mind. I must kill these two bastards or they'll kill me. The swords man is on me. He lunges forward. Without thinking, I side step. Making a fist, I swing for all I'm worth. My fist lands full on his jaw. An excruciating stabbing pain shoots through my fist and up my arm.

'Arghh!' I scream, the pain is intense. A fraction of a second before my fist reached its mark, my foe had turned himself to stone. 'That's cheating, how am I supposed to fight against that?' I look at my hand, the knuckles are torn to shreds and running with blood. I turn to see the other man. He's on his knees, quivering like a frightened mouse.

'What's up with him? You'd think he'd seen a ghost.' Donna's staring at me, mouth wide open.

'What? Why are you looking at me like that? Donna, what's the matter?'

'You, you've turned him to stone! That doesn't happen anymore. We were told stories when we were young, I've never seen anything like it in my life.'

'I turned him to stone?' I could feel myself swell with pride. 'I thought that he'd done it himself. You know a shield sort of thing.' I look towards the other man. He's still trembling on the ground. What should we do with him?

'Please, don't hurt me, I was only following orders.'

'What orders? What were you supposed to do? I ask.

'We were to take Donna back and let you go.'

'He's lying Daddy. They'd never let us get off that easy,' Donna's looking thunderously angry now. She grabs the man by the hair.

'Where's my Mother? What's happened to all the others? What gives you the right to treat us like this?' At this point, he makes a grab for Donna's hand and twists her into an arm lock, with his other arm round her neck.

'If you come any closer, I'll break her neck!' Uncontrolled anger fills my entire being, my blood boils from deep within.

'Let her go!' I shout. For no reason I can understand, he turns to stone as well. To my dismay, Donna's still locked in his grasp, she's choking. Her face, turning scarlet. I must release her from his grip. I rush at them, grab a hold of the stone-man's arm. I pull for all I'm worth, the arm is rock solid. I summon all my strength, with gritted teeth, I wrench the arm clean off the rest of the stone-man's body. Donna falls to the ground, gasping for breath and clutching her throat. I kneel beside her.

'It's Ok sweetie, he can't hurt you now.' I place my arm around her shoulder, only to realise that I still have the other man's arm and hand in my grip. Dropping the stone arm to the ground, I scoop Donna in my arms and hug her. I thought I was going to lose her. I'd vowed that would never happen. Donna's getting her breath back now and returning to a normal colour. She looks me in the eye and punches me full on the bicep.

'What do you think you're doing? They could've killed us! Don't you ever try a stunt like that again!'

'I couldn't help it, I lost my temper, I'm sorry but I did promise to protect you.' Donna throws her arms around me.

'You brave, foolish man, you don't know what could have happened,' then she smiles. 'Thank you Daddy.' We hug for a while, try to gather our thoughts.

'You know they'd have been more use to us in the flesh, at least we could've found out what they know and who else is involved.'

'I didn't mean to turn them to stone, it just happened. Don't ask me how I did it. I just got very angry and Bob's your manikin, two stone figures. What shall we do with them? We can't leave them. We will have to hide them.'

'Let's just drag them in amongst the trees and get out of here.' We get to our feet. I grab a hold of the swords man.

'God, he weighs a ton, we're never going to shift him.'

'Oh come on Daddy. With all your power, you could lift him with one hand.' Feeling rather powerful, I stick out my chest and take a deep breath. Nothing happens. The stone man still won't budge.

'I'm sorry sweetie, I'm just not angry at this moment in time, just relieved. I seem only to have extra strength when I get angry or scared.'

'Daddy, look out, a rabbit!' I spin around.

'Very funny.' I look up to see Donna in fits of laughter.

'I thought if I scared you, you might be able to shift these two.'

'We could drag the little one closer to the swords man, it would look like some mad artist had made a sculpture and put them in the field.'

'Whatever we do, we must do it quick. Faye and Shauna must be in danger, we've to go back and help them.'

'Faye and Shauna are fine,' I say. 'I can sense that they've got everything under control. We must just get you home and safe.' We manage to drag the one armed man closer to the other. I arrange them to look like they've just done battle.

'At least their expressions are right. Pass me the arm, sweetie, it'll look like the sword's man cut it off.'

We sit in the field for a while getting our breath back.

'What now Daddy? How are we going to get home?'

'Well, we have a new car, they were kind enough to leave us theirs, it's the least they could do. Should we keep off the main roads. Can we travel behind the scenes, you could open up the air again.'

'Are you kidding? Your driving almost got us killed. I'll drive. We are staying this side, I don't think you're ready to travel the other side yet, it would be too much for you to get your head round.'

'I don't think much else could surprise me after the last few days. I've become a Daddy again and a sculpture in the space of a day. I can see and feel things, I never even thought of before.'

'That's the Amulet. Remember what Faye said, "Take it slowly." You don't know the powers you have. Remember the saying "power corrupts, absolute power, etc." I don't want you changing. It's you I want to be with, not some super hero.'

'I won't change sweetie, I just seem to have a better understanding of my life now. I don't need to question my sanity anymore. All the things that I thought were in my head, actually exist.'

We walk to the car that was following us, the keys are still in the ignition. Donna insists on driving. I'm glad she does because I'm feeling exhausted. The great strength I felt whilst being pursued, has gone.

'Sorry sweetie, what?' Donna had been talking to me, I had not heard a word she said.

'I said it's not over yet, they'll send others.'

'Who will? What others?'

'The Council, they will send more, they know we are

together. You heard what they said. They were sent to bring me back. Stay awake Daddy, I can't do this on my own.' I have an uncontrollable urge to sleep. The Amulet or the fight have sapped me.

'Open the windows, let the air in. I just can't keep awake.' We open the windows and put the music on loud. Donna is driving. I can see she is nervous by the amount of times she is looking in the rear view mirror. She's chewing on her bottom lip again.

'It's Ok sweetie, nobody's behind us now. Just drive carefully and we'll get home in one piece.'

'We are going to be alright, aren't we Daddy?'

'I don't know, they seem to be determined to get to us. All we can do is try and get back home without any more interruptions. If we stick to the main roads, there will be less chance of being ambushed.'

'I hate them, I hate them! Why can't they leave us alone?'

'They are scared of something. It's not as if we're going to shout from the roof tops, that you're a fairy.'

'It's seven o'clock, Daddy. Faye and Shauna should still be with John. Tune in and see how they are.'

'I'll give it a try.' I close my eyes and focus. 'I'm getting nothing, can't seem to pick her up!'

'Just picture Faye and concentrate.' I close my eyes again, trying to picture Faye, screwing my eyes tight.

'It's no good, I can't see a thing.'

'Concentrate Daddy.'

'I am concentrating! I just can't do it. I can't feel or see her at all. Am I supposed to be getting pictures?'

'I get pictures! If you drive, I'll tune in.'

'You sure you trust me? I don't want to get carried away.'

'Ignore any urges to fly the car.' Donna pulls over, we

change places. Before we drive off I look at her, her eyes have turned white again. This is all going to take a lot of getting used to. As I pull away, I hear little squeaking sounds coming from Donna, the sound a dog makes whilst dreaming. This must be part of the tuning in process. I am driving for about twenty minutes, when suddenly the sky turns black. Snow flakes appear, a little at first but within seconds it's turned into a blizzard. I close the windows to keep out the cold. I can't see to drive. It's April, it shouldn't be snowing!

'I'm going to have to pull over sweetie, I can't drive in this. Donna, I said I'm going to stop.' I pull the car over to the side of the road, turn to Donna. She's in a trance and is unable to hear me. She's still making the funny squeaking sounds. I just sit and wait for her to finish looking for Faye. The snow is getting heavier. If it doesn't stop soon, we'll be stuck.

'Donna have you got through yet?' Still no answer from her. Shaking her shoulder, I get no response.

'Donna, come on, what's happening?' I'm getting worried, she's not responding at all. I'm shaking her hard now, still I get nothing. The snow is building up around the car. This is not right. I must get us out of the car. When I try the door it won't open. I lean past Donna and try her side, her door won't open either. All the time the snow's getting deeper, burying the car.

'Donna, come on, wake up, we're being buried by the snow. We must get out of here.' Sliding my seat back, I kick at the windscreen. Feeling the anger build within. I focus all my energy into my feet, kicking with all I can muster. Still the windscreen doesn't budge. We are entombed in the car, with no way out.

Donna's still in her trance, her eyes white, her face has turned ashen. She's breathing, I can see her breath as it meets the cold air. It's getting colder, the sweat of fear is freezing on my body.

'Donna, please wake up, baby, please wake up!' There's a terrific crashing sound, the car is moving, sliding within the snow. It's completely covered in snow, which has frozen solid around the it. We are sliding, as if stuck in a glacier. The crashing, grinding and screeching getting louder, we are going to be crushed. I try once again to kick at the windscreen but can't move my legs. My arms are as heavy as lead. I look to Donna, a great despair fills my heart. I didn't have time to get to know her, I promised that I would take care of her.

'I love you my sweet little angel, I'm sorry I let you down.' I whisper. The tears leaving my eyes are turning to ice. It's so very dark, I can't keep awake.

'Sorry sweetie, I love you so mu...'

Seventeen.

Cold Shoulders.

I must have passed out. I'm aware that I'm in some sort of cavern, encased in a block of ice. I'm not breathing, I must still be alive as I'm thinking and fully conscious. Through my icy prison I see other shapes encased just as I am. Shapes of people. It's as if we've been put in cold storage, for whatever despicable event awaits us. I can hear muffled sounds, they may be voices, I can't be sure. I try to call out, no sound leaves my lips. I am frozen for some future archaeologist to uncover. It's strange, I don't feel scared. In fact, I'm at ease. The thought of death enters my head, is this death? Is this what happens to us when we end our days? Put on some heavenly supermarket shelf, like a pack of fish fingers.

'Alex, can you feel me? It's me, Faye, Can you hear me?' I become aware of a voice in my head, it's a really strange feeling. I can hear but the voice is from within me.

'Alex, can you hear me? I am trapped too. It's me Faye, Donna is here and Shauna and many others.'

'Faye, is that you? Am I imagining this or are you talking to me? Where are you?'

'I'm not far from you, I am frozen as well. John ambushed us, he knew all along. He was waiting with other Council members, when we got to his place. We didn't stand a chance.'

'What's happened to Donna? Is she here? She tried to contact you. She fell into a trance. Is she Ok?'

'She's here with us, frozen just as we are. Alex, you must try and get free. The Amulet is our only hope. Put all your thoughts into the Amulet, will it to get hot.'

'I can't move, Faye, tell me what to do.'

'Concentrate on the Amulet, tell it to heat up. The heat will melt the ice.' All I can think of is Donna and Faye, trapped in ice.

'Empty your mind Alex, concentrate on the Amulet. If you get out, you'll be able to release us. If you don't, we could be here for thousands of years.'

'Daddy you can do it!' I hear Donna. *Thank God she's Ok.*

'Donna don't worry, I'll get us out of here, I promise.' Clearing my mind of any other thoughts other than the Amulet around my neck. I picture it getting hot, sending its heat through the icy tomb. It's working, I can feel the Amulet getting warmer against my neck and chest. *Fuck! That's burning.* The pain on my chest is intense, the Amulet is burning into my flesh. The melting ice, boiling around the Amulet. I feel the melting ice running down my body. The more I concentrate on heating it, the more it hurts. The ice is cracking and popping around me, sensation coming back into my body. My whole body is cold, all except the burning around my neck and chest. Whoose! The ice that holds me, crashes to the floor, ripping flesh and clothing as it falls.

'Faye, Donna! I'm free, Where are you?' As my vision clears, I see what must be hundreds of people frozen in ice. Nausea fills my body. Row upon row of icy coffins. Every one of them containing a person, fear etched into their faces. How long have they been like this? This is so cruel, why are they like this? Faye and Donna must be amongst them! I call out.

'Where are you? Donna, Faye! Lead me to you, I'll get you out.'

'Keep quiet! You'll give yourself away, you don't have to use your voice. Speak with your mind, we can hear you just as well.'

'Where are you? I can't see which one is you! There are hundreds of people here.'

'Alex, just hold up the Amulet and start melting as many as you can, don't worry about us.'

'Don't worry about you? I have to worry, I love you Faye. I love Donna, I want you both with me.'

'Just start melting, please, you are bound to get us, we are near you.'

'Ok! Ok! I'll do it.' Holding the Amulet, pointing at the nearest ice block to me. I concentrate hard. A beam of blue light, like a lazar, emits from the Amulet. Immediately the ice starts to melt, revealing the prisoner inside. It's not Donna or Faye, I keep melting until the person is free. Again the ice crashes to the floor, flooding the area. A young man emerges, confused and stunned. I move on to the next block, start the melting process over.

'This will take forever, Faye talk to me! Where are you?'

'Stay calm Alex, focus, you can melt them all, think bigger.' Holding the Amulet high, I picture all the ice blocks. The cavern starts to shake. A burning, intense light leaves the Amulet and fills the darkest corners of the cavern. I am finding it hard to keep a hold of it, the heat is burning into my fingers.

'Hold on Alex, don't let go.' Faye's mind is with mine, I feel her strength within. The light is getting brighter, a high pitched screech fills the air. A terrific whooshing, crashing, then the cavern fills with water. I am swept from my feet and driven against the wall by the flood. I look up to see the place filled with dripping, stunned people. Frantically, my eyes search for Donna and Faye. It's impossible to pick them from the crowd, everyone looks the same. Some are standing, some on the floor, flat on their backs. Everyone is confused.

'Alex! Over here,' I hear Faye's voice. I turn to see Donna, Faye and Shauna huddled together, sitting against the wall of the cavern. I rush to them, I can't contain myself, tears of relief stream down my face.

'Thank God, you're safe, I thought I'd lost you, both of you.'

'You did it Daddy, you set us free!' Donna's beaming with pride. 'You did it.'

'We're not free yet,' Faye says. 'We don't even know where we are, we could be anywhere!'

'We seem to be in some sort of cave, are there many caves in the area?' I ask.

'If we're still in Cornwall, there are thousands.' The noise in the cave reaches a deafening level, as people come round from the state of confusion. Some are looking happy, others are crying. The noise is getting louder by the second.

'Well, I think our secret is out, it won't be long before our captors realise we've broken free!' I exclaim, grabbing Donna by the hand. 'We must find a way out, quick.'

'Daddy wait, we can't just leave, we must help the others. Who knows how long they've been frozen? We must all stick together.'

'I just want to get you out of here, come on, the others can help themselves.'

'No, Daddy, that's not like you! All these people are the same as us, locked up, having their lives stolen from them. We must help as many as we can.'

'Can't we just go? I couldn't bear to lose you again!'

'We have more chance of escape, if we all move together,' Shauna adds.

'Alex, this is not you talking. You know we can't leave without the others,' says Faye.

'I'm sorry, I'm just scared of losing any of you, again. You're right of course. Let's make it quick.' Shauna stands, to get the attention of the crowd. I had never really taken much notice of Shauna before now. She's a magnificent looking woman, tall and slender. Long auburn hair, fantastically rich, deep brown eyes. I picture her naked again.

'Hey you! Put your eyes back in your head.' Faye shoots me a look.

'You promised not to read my mind.'

'I didn't have to read your mind, your face said it all.'

'Does anybody know where we are? Hey! I said, does anybody know where we are?' Shauna, calls out to the soggy, dazed mass. People just turn to each other, shrugging . No one has a clue, they are as much in the dark as we are, if not more. Who knows how long we have been imprisoned here.

'Listen everyone, we are all in this together. We need to join forces, if we are to get out of here. This is a Fairy Council prison and you can bet your life, they've posted guards.'

'Who put you in charge?' calls a voice from the crowd. This sentiment is echoed all around the cavern.

'No one's in charge,' Shauna replies. 'We must all take control, sticking together is our only chance. If anyone thinks they are up to the task or has a clue how to get out of here, let them stand forward.' Silence fills the air.

'We must all join hands and surround our selves with a protection shield, there is one amongst us who possesses the Supreme Amulet.' I look to Faye.

'Is that me?'

'Yes it's you, don't let it go to your head.'

'Are you upset? Why are you short with me?'

'I didn't like the way you looked at Shauna. To lose you to The Council is one thing, to lose you to my best friend is another.'

'What? Are you mad? I was looking in admiration, not lust.'

'Sorry, it's just that I've waited so long for you. Can't I be a little insecure?'

'We've got more important things to worry about at the moment, I'm not about to run away. I've only just found you.' I look up to see everyone looking at us. They have all joined hands and are waiting for me and Faye to join in.

'Can you two pay attention?' Shouts Shauna. At that moment, we hear the clattering sound of hurried footsteps, coming from what must be the entrance of the cave. Not everyone is fully conscious, people are still looking confused, scared.

'Alex, you must stay focussed, the Amulet is our only hope,' Shauna tells me.

'We need you at the centre. If we all hold hands, we can concentrate all our energies through you.'

'Through me? Hasn't anyone else got the power, aren't they fairies' with magical powers?'

'They, may not all be fairies', some might be humans just as you are. Anyway it's the Amulet, not you that we need.'

'Can't someone else have it? I can't control the power it has, I might muck things up.'

'Daddy! Quick, hold my hand, here they come!' Running towards us is a swarm of fierce looking men. Dozens of them and they all have weapons in their hands. They are all carrying swords.

'They're an old fashioned bunch, aren't they?'

'They are carrying "Swords of Orfeo." Very powerful magic is contained in them,' Donna says. 'The Amulet might not be enough to stop them.' The cave is now teeming with our enemy.

'We just about out number them. Can't we just charge and over power them?'

'No Daddy, we must draw from the energy from the Amulet.' In our distraction, we didn't notice some Council members had come from behind us. I was grabbed by two men.

'Stop, give up or this man dies,' booms the man to the

right of me, the other holding the tip of his sword to my throat.

'Leave him alone, don't you touch him,' screeches Donna.

'If you hurt him, I will kill you.' My captors laugh at Donna.

'Be quiet little girl, you're already in enough trouble. You and your friends,' says one of the men looking at Faye and Shauna.

'It's Ok sweetie,' I try to reassure Donna. Donna's face takes on an angry expression, her eyes turn white. Reaching her hands towards the men holding me, she lets out a terrific scream. Light radiates from her, enveloping me and my captors. I feel their grip on me loosening. The light and screaming become more intense. My captors fall to the ground. They are dead! I look towards Donna, she is crying, looking afraid.

'What have I done?' she weeps. 'I didn't want to kill them, I just wanted them to let you go.' An eerie silence, surrounds us, people are staring in disbelief. The other swords men are backing away slowly, their faces filled with horror. I walk to Donna and take her in my arms.

'It's them or us,' I say. 'I don't think they would hesitate to kill one of us. They were the aggressors and they got what was coming to them.'

'I've never hurt a thing in my life, I hate violence.' Donna's voice trembles. 'They made me do this to them, why can't they just leave us alone?'

'Come, we must go,' Shauna interrupts. 'They will be back and they will bring others.'

'Come on Donna,' Faye joins us. 'Your Dad is right, they deserved it. Don't blame yourself.'

'Everyone join together, they are scared now. Donna has

shown power that has long been forgotten. If we leave on mass, The Council will be afraid to try and stop us. We must act as one.' Shauna has taken control again. Everyone joins hands, we walk tentatively in the direction we think to be the way out. We use the luciferous quality of the Amulet to guide us through the dank, oppressive cave. The ground under our feet is cold, quaggy. Droplets of cold water falling from the cave ceiling, land on my neck and trickle beneath my shirt. *What the fuck am I doing here? I should be at home on the sofa, watching a Woody Allen film.* People around me are beginning to talk now. They don't seem so afraid. I must admit to feeling safer, being part of something bigger. Faye's grip hurts my hand as she clenches, holding tight.

'How was Donna able to do that?' I ask Faye.

'I don't know, I've never seen anything like it. That sort of power is only told of in stories. Only Orfeo and Tiziana are supposed to posses such magic.'

'This has all gone dreadfully wrong. Why does there have to be this killing? Can't they see what they've done. They are making the same mistakes that have been made for centuries. People can't be kept down, they will always strive for freedom.' Donna is holding tightly to my other arm, sobbing uncontrollably. I have no words of comfort for her. What can I say to her, nothing will ease her pain. *God, why does it have to be this way?*

'Alex, she will be alright. Donna has great strength of mind. She will come to realise that she had no choice.'

'She is so young, she should never know of such things, none of us should.'

'We have tried using words. The Council would not listen. They are the ones who brought violence to their door. They give people no choice but to stand and fight. Just look around at all these people. Who knows how long they have been frozen. That's The Council's answer.'

'Shush!' Shauna calls us to silence. 'Listen, can you hear that?' Everyone falls silent, listening, edging forward slowly, like a vine creeping through a forest. I hear nothing but the stifled breathing of the crowd.

'They are lying in wait, nobody break the circle. We stay together and we are strong.' As we turn a corner in the cavern, we see in the distance, a fleck of light. Voices rise with excitement. Some of the crowd break away and run towards the light.

'Come back! You can't make it on your own. We must stick together.' Shouts Shauna. They don't listen, they carry on running to the light. As the break away group fade into the distance, others call them back. To everyone's horror, a terrible screaming is heard. Those that had run ahead, simply disappear before our eyes. Our captors have no intention of letting us escape without a fight.

'Please, all join hands. Alex, we need you to concentrate on your Amulet. We need it to shield us from any magic thrown at us,' Shauna tells me. As we all join hands, a power uncontrolled, sweeps through my body. I look around, I can tell by the expressions that everybody feels the same. Thoughts, feelings, fears of my allies, fill my head. Some are fearful, mostly I feel the overwhelming need to be free. Anger, at having our liberty stolen from us. I put all my thoughts into the Amulet around my neck, imagining a powerful shield around us all. Donna and Faye are to either side of me. Donna's face still shows the sadness she feels, for what she's done.

'You had no choice, sweetie.' I say, kissing her on the

cheek. 'As I had no choice when I turned the other two to stone, we were forced into it.'

'Why do they make us do this? Why do they make us hate them?'

'They are scared, as scared as we are at this moment. Fear is a destructive force.'

'Alex, concentrate,' Faye grabs me. 'We can ask why, when we are free. You need to put everything into the Amulet now. Don't try and put a reason to their behaviour.' Once again I try to concentrate on the imaginary shield, all the time we're walking cautiously, towards what we hope is the way out. The light in the distance is getting brighter as we get ever closer. Our pace quickens, we're eager to be in the daylight. My head is crammed with the thoughts, excitement of the crowd. With every step the euphoria builds, we can taste the freedom. We know that nothing or no one can stop us. We're an invincible army.

The ground beneath our feet shakes violently, fragments of rock fall from the ceiling of the cave. Some amongst us falter and stumble. Our guiding light goes out, we are engulfed in pitch darkness.

'This is it,' shouts Shauna. A surge of energy takes ahold of us and from our very beings we emit our own light. It's a strong turquoise light, the same as I experienced in Faye's basement. The light reveals our captors. They stand directly in front of us, about ten metres away. In the centre is stood a mountain of a man, holding what looks like a staff.

'Stop or die,' he booms, striking the ground with the staff, causing a thunderous crash, which drives us to our knees.

Screams fill the cavern, people huddle together in fear. I grab hold of Donna, I don't want her out of my sight.

'Whatever happens, don't let go, I won't let anything happen to you.'

'That's Orfeo! He is the most powerful Fairy King. We are lost Daddy, no one can overcome his power.'

'He's a lot bigger than I thought he'd be!'

'That's not his physical presence. He never shows his true form.'

'There is nowhere for you to go,' Orfeo booms. 'If you fight, you die! You, mortal, hand over the Amulet and I will let your daughter live.' I look at Donna.

'Don't do it Daddy, don't trust him.'

'Alex, we can beat them, they're scared,' Shauna tells me. 'If you give it up, we are all as good as dead.' I'm lost, I don't know what to do. I look from Donna to Shauna to Faye. I see that Faye doesn't want me to give up the Amulet.

'How can I believe you. You've imprisoned these people, just because they want to be free. You don't own them. You are not a God, not an aeon. All I see before me is a weak, frightened man. If you want the Amulet, come and get it.'

'You dare defy me little man? I will crush you and all those about you.'

'Leave my Dad alone, we're not scared of you anymore. I would rather die than live a life set out by you!'

'Silence, I am your King. You will bow before me.' At this remark, the crowd explodes. A voice from the crowd calls out.

'You are no King, you're a dictator, a despot. We will take it no longer. I stand by the mortal.' The man turns to his fellow prisoners. 'Are you all with me?' A loud cheer fills the air. The anger burst from Orfeo, smashing the ground with his staff. Bolts of lightning bounce off the walls of the cavern, striking at people randomly. Those hit by the lightning, fall to the ground, dead. To my surprise, the crowd pulls together. Voices fill my head.

'Fight back, use the power of the Amulet!' An immense surge of energy fills me. I focus my thoughts on Orfeo and his hench men. A wave of light radiates from the crowd, hitting our foe. This has no effect on them at all.

'You think your simple powers are a match for mine, fools.' With this, Orfeo points his staff at the people nearest him, turning them instantly to stone. I am overcome by the horror of his actions. Hatred boils from within, I want to kill.

'No!' I reach out towards Orfeo, 'Die you bastard, die!' The cave explodes, sparks, wind and smoke envelope us and our enemy. The sound of a thousand cannon, bursts my ears. Then silence, an eerie, uneasy silence. The smoke clears, all that is left in front of us are a collection of stone figures. After a short period of realisation, people start cheering. On the ground, at the centre of the stone figures is the staff that Orfeo held. I look around, Donna, Faye and Shauna are all Ok.

'We did it, Daddy we are free!'

'It can't be that easy, the fight can't be over,' The adrenalin in my blood wants more. As I calm and gather my thoughts, I walk towards the cold stone statues. Looking into the faces, they don't look like bad men. Then I come across a face I recognise, it's the face of John. A deep satisfaction sweeps over me. Any guilt I had, seeps away. I stoop, pick up the staff.

'Where is Orfeo? I can't see his statue.'

'He was never here in person,' says Faye. 'That was just a projection.'

'Won't he come back with others?'

'I don't think he'll be back, he knows we won't back down. With the Amulet on our side, we are too strong,' Shauna smiles as she says this. 'None of us knew how truly strong it was, until today.'

'You mean, you let us fight without knowing the outcome?'

'You would have fought anyway, even if you thought you'd lose. It's within all of us and today proved it.'

'The way you three looked at me, I thought you knew we would win, that's why I didn't hand the Amulet over.'

'There are no sure things Alex, just faith,' Faye says, flinging her arms around me and kissing me deeply in the mouth.

'Hey, you two, stop it,' says Donna. 'Not in front of the child.'

'You're no child Donna, you've proved yourself a very powerful woman,' Shauna points out. 'Not many amongst us would have stood up to Orfeo in the way you did.'

'That's enough self congratulating, shall we get out of this place?' I hold the staff aloft. 'Does anyone want a walking stick? What no one, I'll have it then.'

We begin again, our bid for freedom, most of us start running towards the light ahead. Shauna, Faye, Donna and myself are running hand in hand. The light looms larger the nearer we get. The air is fresh. I can hear the sea, the waves crashing in the distance. The air has the tang of salt, we are near our goal. I am half expecting another obstacle. Suddenly the cave opens onto a vast stony expanse. My eyes are met by a strange alien world, a prehistoric world. Surrounded by rugged cliffs and rocks. The sky has dark clouds and strange formations, a sky that has just seen artillery fire. We are not on Earth, of that I'm sure.

'Faye, where are we? Is this the Fairy Kingdom.'

'Don't worry Alex, I know exactly were we are. I used to play here as a child. The cave was never here then. You'll be happy to hear, we are in Cornwall. This is Sandy Mouth.' Faye's face takes on a sombre expression. 'I wonder, were all these people trapped in their icy tombs all those years ago? This place always felt magical to me. Was the prison the reason?' As the last of us leave the cave, thunder is heard. We turn to see the cave seal itself. No longer the gaping hole in the side of the Earth, just a small hole about thirty foot up in the rock face with a trickle of water, falling from it.

'Where did the cave go?'

'That is how it looked, when I was younger,' Faye tells me. 'Orfeo is still in control. He may be afraid of us but he is obviously not willing to give up his crown.'

'Do you think we are free yet?'

'As far as I know, most of The Council is sealed up in the cave. I don't think they will try to stop us now, they will have to build up numbers again. That won't be easy as they know we have the Amulet, people will not join them.'

'Daddy, I'm tired. Can we go home?'

'Yes, let's get you back to where you belong. Are you coming Faye, Shauna?'

'I won't be joining you,' says Shauna. 'I think some of

this lot will need help. Who knows how long they have been stuck in there.'

'I'm with you Alex, take me home,' Faye hugs me and Donna.

'Ouch! That hurts,' I yelp.

'Shut up, you big baby,' say Donna and Faye, together.

We make our way up from the sea front, with the rest of the crowd. A pathway leads up between the cliffs. I wonder what we look like to any onlookers, a bedraggled mass of lost souls. Some have a plan as to where they are going, others say they have no place to go. Shauna has taken control. Most are looking to her for guidance.

'How are we going to get home? We have no car, I crashed it in the field.'

'We can take mine. It's only small, then so are we,' says Faye. 'I'm afraid we have along trip back to my place.'

'Will it be safe, to go back to your place?' I ask.

'It should be. All The Council members I know are back in the cave.'

'Good, I don't think I could take any more fighting today.'

'I just want to go home Daddy, I want to forget all that has happened today.'

'Don't worry sweetie, we'll be home soon.'

After about an hour of exhaustive walking, we are lucky enough to hitch a lift from a passing truck driver. He is kind enough to take us as far as St Austell. We all sleep most of the journey.

Eighteen.

Home and Safe?

The journey home was uneventful, compared to the last couple of days. I had become used to so many strange things, I wanted something else to happen. Sad to say, I wanted more conflict. At least another car chase. I have to ask myself, is it me or the Amulet, that hungers for adventure? Faye parks the car outside my house. It's about eight in the morning. Donna calls out excitedly.

'We're home Daddy! Will my sister and brothers be home?'

'I don't know sweetie, we are going to have a lot of explaining to do, when they see you.' As I put the key in the door. A vision of James, flashes before my eyes. He looks distressed. Someone's holding him. He's in pain. In my panic, I fumble with the door key.

'Come on, Daddy get the door open. I want to see my new home.'

'Stay here, something's wrong. James is in trouble.'

'No, Daddy, don't say that.'

'James, Jay. Are you home,' I shout as I run in the house.

'Dad, help! I'm in here.' Rushing into the dining room, from which I hear James calling. I see him sat on a chair with his hands and feet bound with rope. His face is red and wet with tears.

'James! Who did this to you?'

'He did, Dad!' James nods his head, indicating to the right of me. I swing around. Standing tall in the corner, with a look of menace in his eyes, is Smiley.

'Did you think it was going to be that easy?' asks Smiley.

'John, you're dead. I saw you in the cave.' says Faye.

'No, you fucking bitch, that was my brother John, not me.' Spitting venom, 'Now you will all die.' Smiley heaves his mighty sword into the air and swings it towards my head. I see my life flash before my eyes. I had such little time with Donna and Faye. Tears fill my eyes, as I look to them. I see the horror in their faces. Hear their screams of terror. So this is how I end. The screams of my family, hurt my ears. I feel the icy blade against my neck, feel its sting. *Why do I have to end this way. Can't I just have a little more time. Dear God, please, just a little more time.* Before the blade has entered too deep, it and Smiley turn to stone. Hovering just above his head is Faith. She has done this for me. My heart is pumping like a piston.

'Did you do that? Thank you, you're not so bad after all.'

'Yeh, well I didn't want an unhappy ending to my favourite human.'

'Who are you talking to Daddy?' Asks Donna.

'Her,' I say pointing to Faith.

'But there is no one there.' Says Faye.

'Can't you see her? You conjured her up.'

'You're tired, come sit down. I'll get you a tea.' Faye leads me to a chair.

'I'd rather have a vodka.'

'Daddy, its early morning. You can't have a drink this early.'

'Hey! You lot what about me?' shouts James. He's still tied to the dining chair. Donna rushes over and unties him.

'Thanks sis,' says James. Donna, lets out an excited giggle and looks at me.

'How long have you been tied up?' I ask him

'Since yesterday afternoon. That man barged his way in, shouting he was looking for you. Then he pointed his sword at me and said he would kill me if I didn't tell him where you were!'

'Did he hurt you?'

'No, he made me sit in the chair, then he tied me.'

'Thank God, you're alright! Where are Jay and Peter, are they here?'

'What? Jay is here, she just untied me. Peter is due round any time now. What's going on dad? It's freaky Dad. Who was that man, why is he a stone? Why was he after you? Jay, what's going on?' James asks.

'Um, I'm not sure how to say this James, so I'm just going to tell the truth. This is Donna, your other sister.' James, stares at me, dumb struck. 'And this is Faye, a very good friend of mine.' James is still staring at me in disbelief.

'Hi!' Smiles Donna, waving her fingers at James.

'Nice to meet you.' Says Faye, shaking James's hand.

'Ow.' James gets a static shock from Faye. 'Is someone going to tell me, what's going on?'

'We will do our best to explain, I'm not sure I believe it myself.' I look to Faye for help. 'Donna is your half sister, I've only just found out myself.' As I begin to tell James the story of the last few days, the front door opens. In walk Jay and Peter.

'Hi Dad,' says Jay. 'You're back early, thought you said you'd be gone a couple of weeks! You look terrible.' Donna catches her eye. The colour drains from Jay's face. Donna yelps and starts jumping up and down.

'My sister, my brothers, oh, I'm so happy!' Peter, walks into the room. He looks straight at the stone figure, that was once Smiley, and says.

'Oh Dad, what did you buy that stupid thing for? It's rubbish!' Faye, Donna and I look at each other, we burst out laughing. I am just relieved to have all my children safe with me.

Jay, James and Peter took a lot of convincing. At first they wouldn't believe a word of what we told them. Like me, eventually they came around. It's been a month now since we returned home. The house is a little cramped but we are managing. Faith still pops in from time to time, although no one else seems to see her. Jay and Donna are inseperable, spending all their time together. Donna looks very happy, I think she is getting over the events of the recent past. James and Peter, well, they are James and Peter. They seem to be totally unaffected by any of the changes. I am getting used to having Faye around, we are very much in love.

'Shall I open a bottle of wine?' Faye asks. This is the first night we've had to ourselves in a long time. I plump the cushions on the sofa, I'm feeling in the mood for romance.

'That's a good idea, I'll put some music on.' I put a Motown Classics CD into the player, light the candles and lay on the sofa. Faye walks in from the dining room with a couple of glasses, she looks fantastic! *This is it, Alex....This is your lucky night....Let the sparks fly.* Faye places the glasses on the table and sits next to me. We say nothing, she tilts her head to mine and kisses me.

RING! RING! RING!

'I don't belive it.'

'Let it ring, Alex.'

RING! RING! RING!

'I can't, it might be important. It could be one of the children.' I answer the phone.

'Hello!'

'Alex, hi, it's Sarah, how are you?'

'Hello, sis. I'm alright, good to hear from you.'

'Just phoned, to see when you're coming back down. Rob says you owe him a pint.'

'I thought, I'd wait till the summer holidays. I could bring the whole family, there's someone I'd like you to meet.'

'That'd be great. I bumped into Shauna at the weekend. She says Faye's moved in with you? I knew you'd like her. She said she's selling the tea house.'

'Yes, we are starting anew, one big happy family. The children love her.'

'I have some great news too,' squeals Sarah excitedly.

'We can't belive it. We got the results back from the doctor. Rob and me, we're having a baby!'

THE END?